FRIENDS
OF ACPL

W9-BBD-737

THE HAUNTED ISLAND

The
Haunted
Island

by Miep Diekmann

TRANSLATED BY A. J. POMERANS

Illustrated by Jenny Dalenoord

E. P. DUTTON & CO., INC., NEW YORK

First published in the U.S.A., 1961
by E. P. Dutton & Co., Inc.

English translation Copyright, ©, 1959
by E. P. Dutton & Co., Inc., New York
and Methuen & Co., Ltd., London
All rights reserved. Printed in the U.S.A.

FIRST EDITION

No part of this book may be reproduced
in any form without permission in writing
from the publisher, except by a reviewer
who wishes to quote brief passages in con-
nection with a review written for inclusion
in a magazine, newspaper or broadcast.

Library of Congress Catalog Card Number: 61-12455

CONTENTS

CO. SCHOOLS
C529726

CHAPTER ONE

Strange Dream

If only somebody would come by, Matthew thought. A man on a horse, or better still a rider in charge of a whole troop. That would be exciting, Ali Baba and the forty thieves galloping by under the trees!

But there just weren't any horses. It was much too hot for them on the island. It was different for donkeys. There were donkeys on every plantation. Even Brakkeput had two—but they were not used much any more since Matthew's father had bought a small truck to transport the crops to the city. Sometimes Matthew rode one when he was bored and wanted to go on a trip outside Brakkeput.

Oh, it was always the same outside! The dusty wide road which nobody ever used, enormous cacti almost the size of trees, scrub, and in the distance the range of low mountains. Much better to go down to the little bay, with its clear blue water. On the school map it was marked "White Bay," but the islanders who lived beside it, in their squat little houses with the pointed roofs, called it Big Mouth.

This name had obviously arisen because of something that had happened long ago. What it was exactly, Matthew had never been able to find out. Enriqui, who was the best of the storytellers, and who knew the history of every square yard of the island, never said very much when he was asked what was so peculiar about Big Mouth. Nor had Matthew

heard many people ask him. There must be something
terribly wrong if people daren't even ask.

Even Matthew, who was a favorite of Enriqui's, didn't
like asking him. When you did something that Enriqui
didn't like, he would look at you so. . . . In his hideout
among the leaves of the medlar tree, Matthew racked his
brains for the right word. Threateningly? No, it wasn't
that. Enriqui's black eyes, the whites of which looked so
old, so much older than the wrinkles on his brown face,
could never make you feel frightened. Enriqui wasn't like
that at all.

No, it was something altogether different. It was as if he
looked right through you at something far away that only
he could see. Then you had to sit absolutely still and say
nothing, hardly daring to swallow. If you were quiet, nothing would happen, and after a while Enriqui's eyes would
look at you in their usual way again, and then you could be
sure that there was nothing behind you but the trade wind
rustling the leaves in the trees.

I'll just go and have a look at the boats, Matthew thought,
perhaps Enriqui is there. For even if you daren't talk about
Big Mouth, there were still a great many other things you
could discuss with him. The last Harvest Festival, for in-
stance, or the black kid that was so different from all the
other goats. And boats, of course.

What's more, Enriqui always had time to talk to you, no
matter whether he was sweeping out the turkey run, working on the boats where there was always something to do,
or sitting on an upturned kerosene can in front of his house

mending a fishing net. He never seemed to mind your being there. Enriqui was not only a good storyteller, he was a good listener too. Even if you were sure that his thoughts were far away, he always knew exactly what you'd said.

Before Matthew slid down from the medlar tree he looked down from his vantage point to see if Enriqui was in the plantation. But Brakkeput looked quite deserted in the noonday heat. It was only in this tiny copse that there was any shade. The yellow walls of his home, and the terraces around it, seemed to be shimmering gently in the heat. All the shutters were closed, and a stranger might well have thought that the place was empty. But Matthew knew that Mother must be in the living room and Paulina in the kitchen. Father had gone to town. Alfredo and Joseph, no doubt, had seized the chance of a quick nap in the shade, their grubby caps pulled down over their eyes.

The windmills were moving their great arms much more slowly than usual. Even they seemed to be feeling the heat.

When Matthew, his mind made up at last, jumped from the tree, he startled an iguana which scuttled off across the branches. Matthew stood on tiptoe to see if he could see where it had gone. Lucky Alfredo wasn't about, or the lizard would have finished up in his belly. And if Joseph had seen that, there would have been a quarrel, for Joseph maintained that iguanas were poisonous and that you might die if you ate them.

Alfredo and Joseph were always quarreling, and yet they were inseparable.

Matthew kicked one of the medlars that had dropped

from the tree, and sent it flying across the path. He'd just
as soon be at school as spend a holiday all on his own! Why
on earth did Father's plantation have to lie beyond White
Bay, where hardly anybody else lived?

In his school geography book he had read that Brakkeput
was one of the most beautiful spots on the whole of Curaçao.
Tourists would sometimes come and spend a few weeks on
the island to find out just how beautiful.

"It must be marvelous to live here," they would always
say when they met you. "A tropical island . . . !"

You just nodded at them. How could you tell them that
you didn't give two hoots about the romance they all raved
about. Matthew could see nothing romantic in medlars and
papaws, and as for his father's mangy goats and turkeys . . .
well!

He could see why visitors liked going down to the bay
and why they were so keen on sailing with Enriqui in his
fishing boat. Matthew loved boats himself and would have
been happy to go fishing every day, but Enriqui didn't go
out very often—only when Alfredo and Joseph could come
along and they were sure of a good catch. If Matthew was
at home when this happened, he was always allowed to go
with them. And even if Paulina scolded that they had sent
him home filthy again, that couldn't spoil his fun. Mostly he
laughed straight in her face when she sent him to change
his clothes in the washhouse.

"Outside with you! I can't have that smell in the house,"
she would say, shooing him before her to the big water tank
in the yard. And there she'd stand until he'd ducked right
under several times. Then he would be allowed to come out

of the water and put on his slippers, while Paulina rubbed him down with a rough towel. Her calloused hands were so hard on his back that he felt that he was being beaten.

"Them dirty fish," she kept on mumbling.

"You like to eat them yourself," Matthew always wanted to say to her, but he never did, for he knew that Paulina didn't really mean it. She just grumbled as usual.

Paulina's strident voice broke into his thoughts. She was calling Alfredo to come and pump water for her. Matthew began to run. If Paulina caught sight of him and realized that he was looking for Enriqui in the bay, she would call him back. She was always saying there was something evil about the bay—but never saying any more.

Matthew suddenly made up his mind to ask Enriqui straight out. After all, he could simply shut his eyes when he was asking, or just look the other way. He slowed down, not only because it was too hot to run very far, but also because his own resolution frightened him a little.

"Go on," he said softly to himself as he pushed the mangrove branches aside with a quick movement. Almost at the same second he screamed. His yell rang right out across the bay and all over the plantation.

"Matthew?"

Thank goodness, Enriqui was there!

"Enriqui!" Matthew called back anxiously. "Enriqui! Hornets!" He flailed his arms madly to chase them away. Viciously they kept darting from their nest in the mangroves, buzzing furiously, almost driving him mad. He was terrified. "Enriqui! Enriqui!" He couldn't even run for it, for he couldn't see a thing. If he lost his balance, he might fall right into the hornets' nest and then it would be all over with him! "Enriqui!"

Suddenly he felt himself being lifted from behind and carried away. It all happened so quickly that he was still waving his arms about when Enriqui put him down by the white boats on the little beach.

"Let's have a look," Enriqui said. He inspected Matthew's face and arms, his hands, his legs and then his neck. "Well, it's nothing serious," he said.

"I feel as if I've been stung all over," Matthew said, scratching himself violently.

Enriqui slapped him with the brush he was using for painting the boats. A blob of paint stuck to Matthew's hand.

They both burst out laughing. Matthew stretched out his hand to Enriqui as if to say that he'd have to clean it up again, but Enriqui was back squatting on his haunches by the boat and busy painting again.

"I think I'll have a swim. That'll get rid of the itch," said Matthew, looking sideways at Enriqui to see what he would say. For swimming in White Bay was almost as bad as talking about it.

And sure enough, just as he had expected, Enriqui turned on him. "Don't you dare," he said.

"I shan't go out far enough for the sharks," Matthew replied. He pretended not to know what Enriqui was warning him about.

"Sharks!" Enriqui snorted contemptuously.

"Is it *picas* you're worried about?" Matthew persisted,

knowing it was not. *Picas* were water fleas; they were a
terrible nuisance but quite harmless.

Enriqui gave no sign that he had heard. Matthew became embarrassed by his silence and began to rub his hand
awkwardly against the boat. When the paint was almost
off, he climbed carefully into the boat, which was lying
on blocks on the beach, and sat down on one of the narrow
seats. Even though the boat had been well scrubbed down,
it still smelled of fish. Matthew kicked against the kerosene
can by his feet.

"Sit still!" Enriqui ordered from behind him.

Well, at least he had managed to make him say something! Now, if he could only get him into a good temper
again . . . . But before Matthew could think of the next
step, the old man said something very odd, as odd as all the
things that had anything to do with White Bay. "Tomorrow I'm going to put the boats higher up," he said. He said
it under his breath, but Matthew heard him.

"Higher up" meant in the little creek past White Bay.
It was always very difficult to get the boats out of it again,
because it was surrounded by rocks jutting far out into the
sea. And yet Enriqui would rather put the boats there than
on the much wider beach of White Bay. Matthew wanted
to know why.

"This is a much better place for them," he said, by way
of a feeler. He looked around quickly at Enriqui's bent
back. But when Enriqui unexpectedly looked up, Matthew
quickly turned his head away. He stared at the little island
in the middle of the bay: a gray rock on which nothing

ever happened. When the boats sailed out of White Bay, Enriqui always made sure that they kept as far as possible from the island. It had no proper name, but the natives called it Hollow Tongue.

"Let's go and have a look at it," Matthew often said to him. But Enriqui never even bothered to reply.

There must be something odd about that island.

"The boats are all right here, but I'd rather have them up there," Enriqui said. Leaning on the edge of the boat, he got up and put the tin of paint on the seat next to Matthew. Matthew picked up the stick inside it and stirred the paint once or twice.

"Are you afraid something will happen to the boats?" he asked, avoiding the old man's eyes as he spoke.

"Last night I saw a bad man in Big Mouth," Enriqui answered under his breath. Matthew wasn't sure whether he had been meant to hear. When Enriqui "saw" something or somebody "at night," it always meant that he had had a dream which he was sure would come true.

"Where? In the bay?" Matthew asked, his curiosity even greater than his fear of Enriqui's strange look.

"On Hollow Tongue." Enriqui pointed somberly at the island on which no one from the plantation had ever landed. Whoever set foot on it would sink into the ground and disappear forever. The islanders swore this was so, but Matthew found it such an unlikely tale that he could not believe Enriqui took it seriously.

"What would anyone be doing on Hollow Tongue?" he asked, trying to get Enriqui to talk.

"It was a bad man," Enriqui mumbled once more. Then he picked up the paintpot again, and went on working.

"If Father ever gives me a boat of my own, I'm jolly well going to Hollow Tongue, whatever you say," Matthew announced defiantly. He hung over the side of the boat and looked at Enriqui invitingly.

But Enriqui just teased him. "And Enriqui will have to come and rescue you if anything goes wrong? Just like with the hornets!"

"Pooh! Why should I need rescuing?" Matthew said boastfully. "The hornets were quite a different matter."

"You're quite right. If you put your hand into a hornets' nest, you know what to expect, but what do you know about Hollow Tongue?"

"Well, you don't know either! You've never been there, neither has anyone else!" Matthew was triumphant, for what could Enriqui say to that!

"No, I haven't been, that's true, but once upon a time . . ."

At last he's going to tell me, Matthew thought.

But Enriqui bent down again and all Matthew could see was his back.

Matthew would have liked to jump out of the boat and run back home, but Enriqui would have known the reason. Really, Enriqui was maddening!

There was silence for a minute or two. Then Matthew said, "Do you know whether Father's going to give me a boat for my birthday?" For although Enriqui now worked at Brakkeput only when he felt like it, he always knew what was going on. Father often asked his advice, and if one of the natives fell sick, they'd call on Enriqui rather than the town doctor.

"Wait and see," was all the reply he got.

You'd rather I didn't get the boat, Matthew thought, so that I won't be able to go to Hollow Tongue.

When he had made sure that Enriqui was too busy with his work to pay any attention to him, he let his eyes wander over the mysterious island.

A bad man on Hollow Tongue!

Even though he didn't want to believe a word of it, and although the sun was beating down hotly out of a clear sky, he felt a chill running down his spine. Just imagine, just think what would happen if you made fast there and jumped out of your boat—and suddenly somebody pounced on you!

But where on earth could he have come from? Matthew tried to reassure himself.

"All the same, I'll do it," he suddenly said aloud. What a sensation it would cause at school, if he told them he'd been to Hollow Tongue! Piet, who'd once spent his holidays at Brakkeput, had also heard the tales about Hollow Tongue, and he had taken them all quite seriously.

"Matthew, MAAAAtthew!" Paulina's voice rang out across the plantation.

"Father must be back home," Matthew said as he jumped out of the boat. He gave Enriqui a push so that he nearly rolled over.

"Hooligan," Enriqui muttered.

"Enriqui, if I get my boat, I'll take you along to Hollow

Tongue." Rather pleased with himself, he did a handstand, picked himself up off the hot sand and ran off home.

"Just your remember the hornets!" he heard Enriqui call after him.

"MAAAAtthew!" Paulina again.

Matthew ran faster.

The hottest part of the day was over at last, and Brakkeput was coming back to life.

CHAPTER TWO

A Present for Matthew

"Is it big, Father?" Matthew stuck his head just outside the cold shower so that he wouldn't miss a word of his father's reply.

"What do you call big?" said his father, looking at him in the shaving mirror.

With a jerk, Matthew turned off the tap. The last few drops splashed on to the stone floor, then everything was quiet in the bathroom.

"Well . . . er . . ." Matthew wavered. He began to rub his hair, so that Father would think he was too busy drying himself to talk. He was afraid to ask too many questions, but he didn't want his father to know that.

When his father and mother woke him that morning to wish him many happy returns of his twelfth birthday, Father said, "We haven't brought your present along. It wouldn't have gone through the door. Have a quick shower and get dressed. We'll go and have a look at it together. . . ."

And to all his questions: "Where are we going to look?" "What for?" "Is it in the bay or the plantation?" Matthew could get no proper answers. All Father's replies had been evasive, and Mother had just smiled quietly to herself. If only Father had given him some clue. Just imagine counting on a boat and then finding out it was something quite different!

Better not think about it at all, just get dressed as fast as possible.

Barefoot, Matthew ran to his bedroom, where Paulina had put out his clothes. He would have liked to give his father a friendly shove as he passed, but he decided to play safe and give him a wide berth. Father was liable to get cross if you jogged him while he was shaving.

"Come on, I've put out your blue pants and white shirt," Paulina said, as Matthew came in. She was holding the shirt in her hands to help Matthew into it.

"Let go," he said crossly, and snatched the shirt from her. If Paulina had her way, she'd keep on dressing him till he was twenty. "Why must I wear the white shirt today? It'll get dirty in no time!" But he put it on all the same.

All the time he was dressing, Paulina fussed around him, straightening his collar and untwisting his belt. Matthew heaved a deep sigh to let Paulina know how he felt about her, but she just hissed "keep still" between her blackened teeth.

"Well, I hope you've quite done," Matthew growled finally. He turned on his heel and ran back to the bathroom to comb his hair.

"Are you ready yet?" he asked his father impatiently, trying to catch a glimpse of himself in the corner of the shaving mirror.

"Why should I hurry? It's your birthday all day today, and we shan't be cutting your cake until this afternoon."

Now Matthew did give his father a shove, for the shaving was over.

"I say, it wouldn't be a . . . ?" he began, but left his question unfinished. It was better not to talk about it, otherwise something might go wrong.

"No, it wouldn't be a chemistry set," Father said teasingly.

"Couldn't you skip your shower just for today?" Matthew asked, adding, to himself, "so that I can see my present sooner."

"No, I must take an extra long shower because it's such an important day," Father replied, but he burst out laughing when he saw Matthew's cross face.

"You wait, I'll get even with you!" As he ran down the stairs, Matthew thought he oughtn't to have said that. When Father was in one of his teasing moods, there was nothing one could do about it.

Mother was standing by the dining table, quietly arranging sprays of red bougainvillaea in little vases. Everything she did was quiet and peaceful.

Matthew knew the flowers were for his birthday, and he said, because he didn't want to sound too excited, "That's how we get ants in the house!"

"Oh, don't worry about the ants, we'll get rid of them somehow," Mother said cheerfully.

Suddenly Matthew called out, "I know it's a boat, I can see it in your face!"

"You must think that money grows on trees," Mother said.

"Are you starting on me too?"

"Happy birthday to you! . . . Happy birthday to you! . . ." Father sang as he came down the stairs.

"You're out of tune," Matthew called out. He wished Father would stop. That was the worst of birthdays: everybody felt obliged to walk about singing "Happy birthday to you," and when it came to that "hip, hip, hooray" business at the end, you couldn't help feeling that everyone else was just as embarrassed as you felt yourself.

Luckily, Father stopped singing, not because of what Matthew had said, but because at that moment Enriqui stuck his head around the corner of the patio, beckoning urgently. Matthew couldn't make out what he was trying to tell Father, but it was clear that it had something to do with his birthday, for Enriqui kept looking in his direction.

"Perhaps we'd better . . ." Father began. He couldn't finish his sentence, for Matthew had already grabbed his arm and pulled him from the patio.

"Many happy returns, Matthew," Enriqui said.

"Oh . . . er . . . ah . . . thank you very much," Matthew mumbled. Why didn't they get on with it. All Matthew wanted was to see his present as soon as possible.

"It won't be a boat, it won't be a boat," he kept reminding himself, hopping impatiently beside his father as they all walked across the plantation.

They were making for the bay.

"Of course it isn't a boat," he told himself once again. Mother was right, a boat was much too expensive.

Now they had reached the mangrove bush where the hornets had attacked him.

"Look out, now," Enriqui said. Trust him not to forget! Luckily Father hadn't heard. Wouldn't he have laughed if Enriqui had told him about the hornets! Father wasn't

afraid of anything. He even laughed at the dark tales about
Big Mouth and Hollow Tongue.

Matthew would have loved to race down to the beach.
As it was, he had to follow Father and Enriqui slowly down
the narrow path between the mangroves.

He could hear laughter . . . it sounded like Alfredo and
Joseph.

Matthew was walking on tiptoe now, to see better, but
there was nothing to be seen. Normally, the masts of the
fishing boats belonging to Enriqui, Alfredo and Joseph were
sticking out above the bushes, but a week ago Enriqui had
pulled the boats to the creek higher up. It was all because
of the "bad man," though no one else had ever "seen" him.

Matthew could feel his heart beating faster and harder.

"It's because of the present," he told himself. But it was
the same feeling he always got when he came close to Big
Mouth and looked across at Hollow Tongue.

Suddenly, Father, who was walking in front, turned around, put one hand over Matthew's eyes, and guided him with the other hand to the right of the beach. Matthew could easily have looked between his father's fingers, but he kept his eyes shut tight. It must be a very big surprise, otherwise Father wouldn't behave so mysteriously. Perhaps, who knew, it might be a boat after all!

No, he mustn't think of it. They must have reached the water by now. The beach sloped here and this was the place where Enriqui's boat was usually kept.

"Well, what do you think it is?" Father was still covering Matthew's eyes as he asked the question.

"A boat!" Matthew almost said, but he couldn't get it out. Suppose he were wrong? Father might think that he was disappointed with the present he was getting. But what else could it possibly be? What else could be so close to the water? Perhaps it was only a canoe. After all a canoe was a boat too, though not a sailing boat. . . .

"A . . . a . . . a . . ." he began to stammer. Father kept his hand over his eyes.

"Come on, Henrik, don't tease him any longer." It was Mother, who had followed them down. There was someone with her. Probably Paulina. Inquisitive as ever!

"Well, here goes! One, two, three. . . !" Father pulled his hand away.

A boat! It *was* a boat! A real dinghy! A dinghy, a dinghy . . . Matthew would have raced into the water, boots and all, but Enriqui hoisted him on to his shoulders with a mighty sweep of his arms.

"There's no need to get wet," he grumbled. "The boat won't run away."

"Quickly, Enriqui, hurry up! A boat! A real dinghy! Did you know all the time?" Matthew was kicking his legs so impatiently that Enriqui had to catch hold of them.

"Keep still, won't you!" Enriqui was in the water up to his knees when they reached the dinghy. The boat shone golden brown in the sun, and the sail was dazzling white. Above the gaff a pert little flag was flying, and the tiller had been festooned with green medlar leaves.

Carefully Enriqui let Matthew slide down from his shoulders on to the little seat. Then he waded back to the beach to join the others and get a good look at Matthew in his new boat.

"Can I go around the bay just once?" Matthew called.

"Do you have to ruin your clean clothes?" Paulina shouted crossly.

"Have your breakfast first," Father said.

Mother was waving to him and smiling, Matthew saw.

So were Alfredo and Joseph, whom he now saw for the first time that morning. It must have been they who had rigged up the boat and anchored it here.

He would have liked to . . . he would have liked to do everything at once, yelling and shouting and calling out mad things, and singing at the top of his voice. Just to let them know how happy he was. But all he could do was to sit still on the little seat, his hand on the tiller, and look up at the sail and the little pennant. The pennant was red, white and blue, and the number of the boat was clearly printed on the sail. "H55" its large letters proclaimed proudly.

He'd have to do something, he couldn't just sit here! Matthew got up carefully and, holding on to the side of the boat, felt his way for'ard. He'd have liked to sit in the bows to admire his boat from that angle. But not knowing how the dinghy would behave, and because the others were still looking at him, he decided to do nothing.

At heart he was glad when he saw Enriqui coming back for him through the water. If he hurried over breakfast he might still be able to go once around the bay before school.

"I've never had such a wonderful birthday!" he shouted across to his mother and father while he was still on Enriqui's shoulders.

"I wonder whether we really ought to let you sail by yourself on Big Mouth?" Father teased as they walked back to the house.

"Oh, go on, Father!"

"Well, be sure not to go to Hollow Tongue! Or else Enriqui won't have a moment's peace!" Father slapped Matthew on the back so hard that he nearly fell over.

"As long as you stay inside the bay, it's quite all right," Mother said.

"Of course I will," Matthew promised at once. A thought suddenly struck him, and he raced home ahead of his parents, so that he didn't hear Mother saying to Father, "Let's hope that the boat will make him feel less lonely. There's so little for him to do on the plantation. We are so terribly isolated."

"He's never complained, has he?" Father asked. "He's just as fond of Brakkeput as we are!"

"Mr. Van Rooy, sir," Enriqui broke in. "Please tell

Matthew he mustn't go to Hollow Tongue." Enriqui's face
was so grave that Father didn't have the heart to laugh.

"Have you been seeing things again, Enriqui?" he asked.
Enriqui nodded, without saying just what he had seen.
He knew perfectly well that Matthew's father paid no at-
tention to any of the tales that went around the plantation.

"I should think all your ghost stories will have made him
so scared that he really won't dare."

The sound of the gong reached them from the house.
When they got to the house, Matthew was waiting for his
parents with a little packet in each hand. It was a family
custom that anyone who had a birthday bought presents
for all the others.

"Oh!" said Mother, as she opened her parcel. "How
clever of you to remember!" She held out the leather case
for Father to see. "It's for my sunglasses, you know."

"You lost yours a long time ago, didn't you?" Matthew
said proudly.

"And a new thriller for me!" Father opened the book
and glanced at the chapter headings. "That'll keep me
awake at night!"

"You can change it if you've read it," Matthew said
quickly, "but they told me in the shop that it's only just
out and that it's one of the best thrillers ever."

"Thank you very much, Matthew. I wish it were your
birthday every day!" Father made as if to jab him with the
book, but Matthew was too quick for him.

"If we finish early, may I just go once around the bay,
in my dinghy?" How wonderful it sounded: "my dinghy"!

Matthew saw that his mother was undecided, and quickly looked at his father.

"Hadn't you better wait until this afternoon? You'll have to change your clothes twice otherwise, and you haven't really got time." The tone in Father's voice was not one that Matthew wanted to argue with, and he dropped the subject.

"You read your birthday letters," Mother said, to take his mind off the boat.

"I'll have to answer every single one," Matthew grumbled, pulling a face. He was so excited that he could hardly open the envelopes.

"Who's taking me to school today?" he asked when breakfast was over. "Alfredo or Joseph?"

"Neither. We're taking you on our way to the shops."

"Hooray!" Matthew jumped up from his chair. "Will you be coming to fetch me too?"

"No. Piet's mother is bringing you back together with Dick and Tim. Oscar, Jan and Victor are coming later with Aunt Else and Nicky."

"Why Nicky? She'll be the only girl!"

"Nicky is your cousin," Mother said, "and what's more she's as wild as Piet and Tim put together, and that's saying something!"

"She'll want to come in the boat and order us all about."

"They all will," Father said. "In any case, no more than three in the boat at one time, is that clear?"

Matthew nodded meekly. If he had his way nobody at all would be allowed in his boat just yet.

You had to get to know a boat very well before you could tell exactly how she would behave. Matthew had never sailed alone before. Just imagine if he made a fool of himself in front of the others! Still, it would be very nice to show them that he had a boat of his very own. And after all, she shouldn't make things too awkward for him. There was only one sail and no centerboard. And he had often been allowed to steer the big boats all by himself, while Enriqui was busy hauling in the nets.

"Well, it's time to go to school," Father said, getting up from the table.

What a bore school is, Matthew thought. But in the car, on the way to Willemstad, the capital of the island, he became more and more cheerful. He thought of dozens of ways of announcing the news to the people at school. The important thing was not to sound as if he was showing off. Otherwise Gerard de Wit, whom nobody liked, would be sure to start shouting, "Daddy's little sprout!" He called Matthew that because his father had a market garden on the plantation.

"That's one person who *won't* come in my boat," Matthew promised himself.

"Have you thought up a name for her?" Father asked, looking at Matthew in the driving mirror.

"No, I haven't yet. What do you think of . . . ?" Matthew frowned as if he were concentrating, but in fact his brain wasn't really working. A name . . . odd, wasn't it? A boat had to have a name . . . he must have time to decide . . . there was no hurry . . . it would be fun just thinking about it. . . .

Father set him down outside the school. Matthew quickly said, "Good-by," but didn't wave. Piet and Tim were coming, and waving was rather babyish.

He could see the girls standing in a circle and singing one of their silly songs.

"Hello, Matthew!" Piet and Tim came up on either side of him to wish him a happy birthday.

"Hello," Matthew said.

"Well?" The boys looked at him expectantly.

"I've been given a dinghy!" None of his carefully-thought-out speeches could have made a greater impression.

Piet whistled expressively, and Tim shouted to the others, "Matthew's got a dinghy!"

The girls broke up their circle, and gathered around Matthew. His other classmates came running across the yard.

And until the bell rang, Matthew had to answer so many questions, and to promise so many of his friends that they could come sailing with him, that his head was spinning.

"I suppose your father just bought the leaky old tub that belonged to the Blue Water Inn and had it painted up," Gerard de Wit said spitefully, as they went into the classroom. Matthew turned on him, but Piet had already given Gerard a punch on the jaw that sent him sprawling.

Piet was sent to the headmaster and kept out of the first lesson, and Gerard was sent to get himself a drink of water. When he came back, he sat down at his desk which was just behind Matthew's and hissed, "Daddy's little sprout in a leaky old tub, just like Moses in his basket! Mind you don't sink—" He got no further, for Anja Vermeer, who sat behind Gerard, gave him a sharp kick under the bench.

"Have you quite finished?" the teacher said acidly. But, for the rest of the lesson, nobody was really concentrating on French irregular verbs. After all, Matthew was in their class, and they all felt that gave them a share in his boat.

CHAPTER THREE

On the Island—for a Second!

Matthew heard footsteps and voices behind him and looked up anxiously. He started to put down the tin of white paint and the brush, but changed his mind. The voices were too near. Still squatting on his haunches, he hopped to the left of the beach. He looked around to see if he could get any farther back, but he was almost touching the boat. If he wasn't careful, he'd fall against the wet letters which he had painted with so much care on his dinghy.

"Hi, Matthew!" Alfredo used one finger to lift the edge of his cap. That was his way of saying "good morning." Joseph, who was with him, just grinned. Matthew could never understand why the twig that he was forever chewing didn't drop out of his mouth. It was always there, and Matthew always looked at it convinced that one day it really would fall out.

"Well . . . ?"

Well, what? Matthew thought, but he knew what Alfredo meant. Had he found a name for the boat, and what was it?

Matthew stared at them, saying nothing. Perhaps if he did not answer they would go away. But Alfredo and Joseph didn't budge.

Matthew squinted pointedly over their shoulders at the plantation. "That's where you ought to be," he seemed to be saying, "not here. If Father only knew." But of course he couldn't say it out loud. They would just laugh and say something like: "You and your father, we don't need either of you to tell us what to do. If we want to stay in the bay, in the bay we'll stay. The corn and the sugar canes will grow perfectly well without our gaping at them all the time."

I hope you're comfortable, Matthew thought, as Alfredo sat down on the beach in the shadow of the boat, leaning his head against the block on which the boat was resting. When Alfredo had found a position that suited him, Joseph sat down next to him. He was too easygoing even to find a comfortable place. Alfredo usually had to do it for him.

Still squatting on his haunches, Matthew turned to face the two men. He had such cramp in his calf muscles that he nearly lost his balance. And still he dare not get up. First he must see what the two would do.

Alfredo pulled his cap over his eyes, and Joseph covered his face with his handkerchief. Only the twig could be seen sticking out from his teeth.

If only they would stay like this for a bit, Matthew thought, but he knew perfectly well that they wouldn't. Soon, Father would return to Brakkeput, and they'd have to pretend that they'd been working hard all day.

Without making a sound, Matthew put the paintpot on the sand, placed the brush across it and got up carefully. He kept close to the boat. If they should look up suddenly, they wouldn't be able to see anything.

But Alfredo and Joseph did not look up.

As if he were interested only in the bay and the moun-

tains on the other side of it, Matthew pretended to gaze aimlessly over the top of his boat. But he was really looking at something quite different: the name which he had just painted in white letters on the bow. He knelt down so as to get a closer view. The letters looked rather good. They were just the right size and the spaces between them were even.

It had taken him two weeks to make up his mind to start. Everybody on the plantation thought he was short of ideas, but there had never been any doubt in his mind about what

to call her. Only what would the men say about it? Hadn't
Alfredo and Joseph laughed at him when he had insisted on
names for his father's donkeys? They would be sure to
think naming a boat was just as funny. Their own boats
simply had a number. He could imagine them for days to
come, having a wonderful time yelling the name right
across the plantation.

That was one reason Matthew had hesitated so long. And
besides he wanted to get in some practice before actually
painting the name on the boat. Every afternoon, as soon as
he was far enough from the plantation, he had tried his hand
at it on a plank.

And just today when he had at last decided to take the
plunge, these two had to come and get in his way!

Matthew looked over at Alfredo and Joseph. He realized
that Alfredo was watching him intently under the peak of
his cap, and he straightened up. His hands in his pockets, he
took a step backward. And when he saw how splendidly
the wet letters stood out against the light brown wood, he
was suddenly past caring what Alfredo and Joseph might
say. Anyway, he'd give them what-for if they dared to poke
fun at the name.

Alfredo dragged himself to his feet, and Joseph followed
his example. Their thumbs stuck in their belts, they came
and stood next to Matthew. Before they could open their
mouths, Matthew said, "The paint's still wet, look out!" as
if this might somehow stop their reading it.

"ELINE!" Alfredo said the name out loud. He nudged
Joseph. Matthew was afraid to look at them, for he was

sure that Joseph would start grinning, as he always did. But there was no sound. Joseph was nodding approval.

Alfredo had taken off his cap and was thoughtfully scratching his head. "A good name," he said finally.

Not, "a nice name," but, "a good name."

"Can he possibly know whom I named the boat after?" Matthew asked himself.

"Eline! Your mother!" Joseph was still nodding.

How did they know that was Mother's name? Had they heard it from Father? Or did they talk about her among themselves? If it came to that, what did Alfredo and Joseph talk about at home?

"Come along now," Alfredo jerked his head at Joseph who turned obediently and followed him up the path to the plantation. Matthew watched until they were almost out of sight.

"Be careful with the *Eline* . . . the Big Mouth. . . !"

Careful? Of what?

What could possibly happen to him now that his boat was called *Eline*?

CO. SCHOOLS
C529726

Still panting from running so hard, Matthew reached the beach. He was just in the nick of time, too. Really, Mother might have told him that Aunt Else and Nicky were coming this afternoon. As soon as he had heard their car draw up outside, he had vaulted out of his bedroom window. He started to run when he reached the patio, and he ran right across the yard and around the turkey run into the plantation. That was one place where Nicky wouldn't look

for him; the turkeys gave her the creeps, with their naked
necks and their feathers crawling with lice. She was calling
him now, but Matthew did not answer.

She can shout till she's red in the face, he thought to
himself. But what if she came down to the bay to look for
him in his boat? He had to get there first. Once he was
afloat, he could simply pretend not to see her.

Trust Nicky to turn up just after he had christened the
boat, when he particularly wanted to go out alone.

There was no time to see if Enriqui was anywhere about
to help him push the boat into the water. He groaned under
the strain, for it was torture to pull the *Eline* from the
blocks. "One, two, and *heave!*" he muttered. And once
again: "*Heave.* . . ." But the boat wouldn't budge. If only
Nicky didn't . . .

Luckily, he made it, and as soon as the boat was in the
water, he leaped in. He fell against the side, but he was in
too much of a hurry to care. Never before had he hoisted
the sails so quickly. From habit, he looked up at the little
pennant to see which way the wind was blowing. But its
direction never changed in the bay; it was always northeast.

He felt behind him for the tiller, holding the sheet in
one hand. As he sat down he looked quickly at the beach.
No sign of Nicky yet. Even so, it was best to get across the
bay as fast as possible. The farther out, the safer he was.

Should he pass Hollow Tongue, or sail around it? Once
he was behind the island, Nicky would never spot him.

He had never before set course directly for the mysterious
rock in the middle of the bay, and he had a hard time holding

the boat into the strong trade wind. As he tried to round the little island, he was nearly dashed against the rocks. He had come about too quickly. The sail was flapping dangerously, and Matthew had a moment of panic. The boat was out of control.

At that moment he forgot all about Nicky, but remembered Enriqui's warning. What if the natives were right and his father wrong to call all their stories about Big Mouth and Hollow Tongue "utter rubbish"?

Matthew closed his eyes tight, hauled on the sheet and pushed against the tiller until suddenly he felt the sail filling with wind. Quickly he opened his eyes again, and then threw his full weight to the right because the *Eline* was heeling dangerously.

Everything happened so quickly that he hardly realized that he had sailed right around Hollow Tongue and was facing the beach again. It wasn't until he had recovered from the shock that he suddenly remembered why he had wanted to get to the other side. To hide from Nicky!

Well then, he must get there somehow.

Sail around once more? And take another chance with those rocks? If only he could remember exactly how he had maneuvered the boat.

"MAAAtthew! . . . MAAAtthew!" he could hear in the far distance.

Quickly, come about! Keep well clear of the rocks and then turn! It was lucky his dinghy was so small and the water so deep right close to the rocks.

It worked, it worked! He could have shouted for joy.

Nicky was yelling louder than ever. Matthew wasn't too happy. Still, if Mother or Father told him off for leaving her standing like that, he could tell them that he'd been much too busy trying to round the island; and so he had been. And Father would see that he hadn't been frightened by any of the stories about Hollow Tongue.

Carefully, Matthew ran the *Eline* close to the island. Here there was a spur of rock to which he could make fast. Only he'd better shorten sail, for the wind was too strong to be trusted.

Well, here he was. Now Nicky couldn't spot him, although she might just be able to see the top of the mast and the pennant. In any case, he couldn't see her.

But after a few minutes of sitting dead still on the bottom of his dinghy, his cousin's shouting began to bother him again. "I can see you, Matthew!" her voice rang out over the bay. "I'm going back to tell your mother. . . ."

Matthew wasn't taken in. Nicky was a horror, and she could fight like a cat, but she wasn't a sneak. That he knew perfectly well, and it made him feel even worse. If only he could do something else . . . read a book, or . . . or . . . He looked around for something to distract him from the voice echoing across the water, and his eyes came to rest on the little island. Only then was he completely aware where he really was.

Right next to Hollow Tongue! Almost on Hollow Tongue! He had managed not to look at it, not to know it was there, but—he was on Hollow Tongue!

It was absolutely still now in the bay. Nicky must have

given up. He was too far out even to hear the windmills on the plantation. The water and the leaves of the palm trees moved soundlessly.

Suddenly his boat scraped against the rocks. Matthew leaped to his feet.

I must keep her off! he thought. She'll get smashed! He looked around, though he didn't really hope to find anything he could use. He could hardly believe his eyes when he saw some thick sun-dried branches. Yet there were no trees on Hollow Tongue!

Without thinking, he put one foot out of the boat. But he jumped back at once. Something had moved! He had seen a shadow in a crack in the rocks. Something was lying there waiting for him.

This was it! Anyone who dared to set foot on Hollow Tongue would be swallowed up by the ground. Enriqui had said so.

Matthew wanted to scream, to yell . . . to let someone at home know where he was. But he could not make a sound. At that moment he heard Nicky's voice again. "Matthew . . . MAAAtthew! You must come back. Your father wants you!" Without looking where he put his feet, he climbed up the rock. They must see him! They must know he had been there! IT wouldn't dare to touch him now while people were watching.

"Hallo, halloooh!" he called unsteadily, waving both arms. Now he could see them: Nicky and his father and Enriqui, and Alfredo and Joseph coming up behind at a jog trot. Father made signs to him to come back at once.

"I'm coming. . . ." The words brought his courage back. He took a good look at the island. When he got back, Alfredo and Joseph were sure to ask him what Hollow Tongue had been like. He'd never let them know how scared he'd been. He'd make them think he'd seen the whole island.

To tell the truth, it was rather exciting to stand on this flat piece of rock in the middle of the sea. The ground was beautifully even, except for the crack in the middle. . . . But that was only a couple of feet wide. Anyone could jump over that.

Matthew looked up again to make sure the others were still there. Then he took a big step right across the crack. He grinned as he saw a couple of crabs scuttling away. That's what he must have seen before. How silly to have been frightened by something like that! Lucky no one had been there to notice!

His hands were still trembling as he hoisted the sail, and he had difficulty in casting off. But when, a few minutes later, he ran the boat up on the beach, he felt perfectly calm.

"Golly, how did you have the nerve?" Nicky greeted him with admiration.

Enriqui, Alfredo and Joseph said nothing. Their faces were somber.

"Oh, it was nothing," Matthew replied, but he meant it more for the men than for his cousin.

"Well, sir, your boat certainly looks in fine shape," his father said.

"Yes, sir," Matthew said, cheeking him. "Next time I'll take some old tires along so that I can land properly."

And, afraid that his father might have something more to say to him, he turned to Nicky and said, "Well, are you coming?" He winked by way of encouragement.

Slowly, Nicky took off her shoes and socks, threw them into the boat, and waded out.

"For goodness' sake, not to that stupid island," she said as Matthew pushed out.

"Well, as it's you. . . ." Matthew pulled a face as if it was a tremendous sacrifice she was asking him to make. In his heart he blessed her timidity.

When they had gone a little way out, he looked back to the beach. His father was no longer there. Alfredo, Enriqui, and Joseph were still standing, still saying nothing.

CHAPTER FOUR

Five Men Escape

"I saw it myself, I tell you!" Nicky gave Piet a push because he looked so disbelieving.

The others, standing in pairs around the playground, egged them on, "Go on, Piet, don't let her get away with it!"

But the last thing Piet wanted was to have a fight with Nicky. He had other things on his mind. Matthew had been on Hollow Tongue! And he had not just landed and left again, he had actually pitched a tent there. Every afternoon after school, he would sail out, do his homework there, and stay until suppertime.

Piet looked searchingly at his friend. If Gerard de Wit made claims like that, you knew just where you were, because he was such a terrible boaster. But Matthew!

Matthew saw everyone was staring at him. He tried to look unconcerned, and tried not to see Nicky grinning proudly because he was her cousin. They were all expecting him to say something. If he simply said, "Oh, there's nothing to it," they would think he was showing off. So he gave a little cough, and shrugged his shoulders nonchalantly. "It was quite a job pitching the tent on the rock," he began.

"Can you sleep in it?" asked Anja Vermeer.

"He's put an air mattress in it," Nicky answered for her cousin. "And there's a box inside to sit on, and lemonade . . ."

"It's just like Robinson Crusoe," Anja broke in.

"Have you been in the tent, too?" Piet asked Nicky.

"No, thank you." Nicky shook her head. "Wild horses wouldn't drag me there."

"Just listen!" Tim snorted contemptuously.

"You wouldn't dare either," said Nicky, furious at being jeered at in front of all the others. And by Tim of all people! No one had ever noticed anything specially brave about Tim!

"It's quite an ordinary island," Matthew insisted; but the quiet way he said it impressed his classmates even more.

"And what do you do when you get there?" Gerard de Wit asked him.

Matthew looked at him suspiciously.

"I've told you, he does his homework," Nicky spoke up again. Matthew was never one for quick answers, she knew, and she wasn't going to let that awful Gerard drive him into a corner.

"He does his homework, he does his homework. . . ." Gerard chanted mockingly. "Why does he need a whole island just to do his homework? I shan't believe it till I see it . . ."

"Clever Dick," Anja cut him short. "You're just jealous, that's all!"

"What would *you* do on the island?" Tim asked. He winked at the others.

"That would be telling!"

"You just don't know, that's all," Nicky said. She was itching to hit Gerard over the head. He was her pet hate but she was a little scared of him. He would never fight back, but he usually got his revenge later with some nasty little trick or other.

"There's the bell, everyone!" Anja called. She snatched up her satchel and rushed for the school door.

"Hey, wait a minute, all of you!"

Victor! Why was he so late? They'd been so excited that they hadn't even missed him.

"Listen," he panted, breathless from running. From the tone of his voice they could all tell that he had terribly important news.

"Come on, break it up!" That was the caretaker.

"I'll tell you inside," Victor gasped to his classmates.

In the end they had to wait until the first break because he wanted to make sure of telling them all together. Piet, who was next to him, whispered the whole story of Matthew and the island, but Victor did not seem to be particularly interested. Piet was as hurt as if he himself had been slighted. But when, at break, Victor told them his own news, Piet knew why.

"It's just like a story out of a book," Matthew said himself; and his own adventure seemed tame by comparison.

"Did I understand you to say—?" Mady began, in her funny voice. She wasn't very quick on the uptake, but she was very warmhearted and never said anything unkind about anybody. So everybody liked her all the same.

This time Victor was rather glad that she hadn't understood, because it gave him an excuse to tell it all over again.

"Actually, it's still a secret," he explained. The others nodded solemnly.

Victor's father was Commissioner of Police for Curaçao and its five neighboring islands. All Victor's stories about his father's work were secret, since anything he picked up was not intended for his ears. His classmates understood that perfectly well. Sometimes he would tell them about a strike that was brewing, or about a ship that was smuggling opium and that had been boarded by the police in the Bay of Willemstad. Or what some drunkards had screamed at each other in the cells. But this morning's story capped the lot!

"Five convicts escaped from Uquique a few days ago in a small dinghy! A couple of them are sick, I think. In any case they haven't got enough food or water to get very far. They may try to land here to take in water and food. And then we shall have to hand them over and they'll be sent back to prison. That's what 'the authorities' say."

"And will your father have to do what they say?" Piet asked anxiously.

"There's nothing else he can do," Victor said, a little offended. "If the authorities say he must do it, then he must do it."

"And a criminal is a criminal," Anja said, rushing to Victor's defense.

The others were too astounded to say anything.

"Yes, but . . ." Piet did not give up so easily.

"Yes, but what?" said Victor aggressively. He was none too happy about it himself. That morning, when he had overheard the news at home, he had felt the same as Piet.

"Haven't you ever heard what the jail in Uquique is like?"

Piet asked. "Everyone knows about it! No one has ever managed to escape from it before. It's between a steep cliff and a deep bay. You can almost touch the water through the bars, and the water's always full of sharks. The prisoners throw their scraps into the bay and that attracts them. If you try to reach it from the sea, the sharks will capsize your boat, and before you know where you are, they've gobbled you up."

"How awful!" Nicky said, shuddering.

"How on earth did the five men manage to get away, then?" Matthew asked.

Victor shrugged his shoulders.

"And how on earth do you get hold of a boat if you are in prison . . . and water and food for the journey?" Tim wondered.

"Somebody must have helped them, of course," Victor continued.

"In that case they couldn't have been very bad criminals," Mady said sweetly.

"Someone told me that in Uquique innocent people are thrown into jail just because the government doesn't like them. They are always having revolutions there, and each time there's a new set of prisoners. They aren't *bad* people at all, really—just people who have different ideas from the government." Piet nodded vigorously, by way of emphasis.

"Victor . . ." Matthew was wondering whether it was safe to go on. Victor had a very quick temper, though it never lasted long. "If these men *should* land on Curaçao, couldn't your father pretend he hadn't seen them?"

"Why don't you ask my father that?" Victor replied testily. It was just what he'd been thinking all morning, but he wasn't going to say so.

"But if someone saw them and took them to the police station, how could Victor's father say he hadn't seen them?" Jan Dikkers said with inexorable logic.

"But why should anyone know that they're wanted?" Piet asked.

" 'WANTED' notices are being plastered all over the island this morning," Victor explained gloomily. He shrugged his shoulders, as if to say there was nothing he could do about it.

"Then let's tear the notices down," Nicky said aggressively.

"All over the island?" said Matthew.

No, that wasn't possible, they all realized that.

"Perhaps they won't land here after all. Perhaps they'll just pass us by," Piet said hopefully.

They all sighed with relief.

"Father says they'll have to land here. They've got to get food and water, and they'll just have to get the sick ones out of the scorching sun. Otherwise they're done for." Victor whistled between his teeth.

"Oh gosh. . . ." The others looked worried again.

"Matthew. . . ."

They all looked at Matthew, as Piet said his name. And although nothing else had been said, Matthew felt himself flushing for he knew perfectly well what was coming.

"You must go out to meet the men in your boat and warn them off."

"And make sure that they have enough water and food so that they can go on," Nicky added.

Matthew looked at Victor pleadingly. It was easy for them to talk. *They* didn't have a boat. *They* didn't have to do anything.

"Look, I'll come with you," Piet said persuasively. "We'll make up some excuse so that I can stay with you for a few days."

"Then you'll have to skip school as well," Victor remarked. "You don't suppose it'll be enough just to watch for them at night?"

"We don't even know which part of the island they'll make for," Matthew began weakly.

"They certainly won't come in from the north. They couldn't land anywhere along that coast without being dashed against the rocks. And even if they managed it by the skin of their teeth, they'd never be able to get away again. Not a single ship has ever brought it off in the whole history of the island."

"Well, they might sail so far to the south that I couldn't get out to them."

"In any case, your mother won't let you sail out of the bay," Nicky said.

Well, that was a bit thick. "That doesn't matter!" Matthew said quickly. He didn't want to be a laughingstock. That was scarcely the right kind of excuse. "I don't even know what their boat looks like. I can't go out to meet any old boat that happens to sail by, and in any case my father would notice straight away that my boat was missing. How on earth can I skip school like that without being found out?"

"The whole idea's a lot of nonsense, anyway," Victor said suddenly. "Just imagine Matthew actually doing it and then being found out. They'd throw *him* into Marietje instead of the convicts."

They all laughed. "Marietje" was a cell on a lonely reef reserved for hardened criminals.

There was relief in their laughter, too. Matthew didn't have to be afraid now that the others would take him for a coward, and Victor didn't have to worry about betraying his father. And the others were glad that no one could accuse them of just standing by while Matthew and Piet took all the risks.

The only one who didn't laugh was Gerard de Wit. He said derisively, "What a fine pair of heroes!"

"Shut up, you squirt!" Nicky shouted.

"Well, what would you do?" Matthew asked. He wasn't going to take that lying down. After all, he was practically the discoverer of Hollow Tongue, so he didn't have to put up with any nonsense from such a silly fool.

"Well, if *I* had a boat . . ." Gerard said sneeringly.

"Come on, tell us!" Nicky shouted indignantly.

"You don't suppose Matthew's going to be stupid enough to lend you his boat?" Tim yelled, ready to fly at Gerard's throat. The two had been bickering all morning, and he was spoiling for a fight.

Piet said, "Oh, don't take any notice of him." But Tim shook him off and advanced toward Gerard.

"Oh, stop it, you two," Mady said, "it's much too hot to fight, and you'll be caught anyway. What good will it do?"

"I say, look!" Victor was pointing straight ahead. At first, Matthew thought he was just trying to distract Gerard.

"Where?" Nicky asked impatiently.

"What did I tell you? Look at that sidecar!" Victor put two fingers in his mouth and gave a piercing whistle. The police sergeant standing by the motorbike looked up and waved.

"That's Hemmes," Victor told the others, "from Abau police station."

"And who's the other one?" Anja asked curiously. Like everyone else she was standing on tiptoe to see what was happening across the road.

"One of the deputies, I suppose."

In dead silence the children watched the two men at work. They didn't have to ask Victor what they were doing—they could see for themselves. The man with the sergeant was plastering the wall opposite the school with a big placard giving the names and descriptions of the five fugitives from Uquique. And the sergeant was standing by to see that he did his work properly.

"They're not wasting any time, are they?" Nicky said.

The others nodded, not daring to look at one another. They all had the feeling that the fugitives were as good as lost. If only Victor's father had been able to stop them from putting up the "Wanted" notices. . . .

Victor guessed what they were all thinking. Staring hard at the ground, he kicked a stone out of the way. He only looked up again when he heard the sergeant start up the motorbike. Hemmes waved to him and the other man waved his paste brush. But Victor didn't wave back. He clenched his fists in his pockets.

"On the orders of the Big Chief himself . . ." Gerard de Wit began but he got no further, because Victor went for him the moment he opened his mouth. He had had it coming to him all morning.

"Victor, look out! Simons!" Nicky called out. She had seen the English teacher coming toward them.

Matthew and Piet used all their strength to drag their friend off Gerard de Wit, then as if nothing had happened they ran with him to the other side of the playground. Gerard alone stayed behind.

"Well," said the teacher, "what's been happening here?"

"They've been fighting, sir," a few boys from the lowest form volunteered readily.

"Yes, I can see that," Mr. Simons replied, as he inspected the bruises on Gerard's face.

"They're always picking on me, sir, and just because I . . ." But Gerard did not finish his sentence. The teacher had seen the notice. A few steps and he was at the gate, with Gerard trotting beside him.

"It's about the criminals from Uquique, sir," he said.

The teacher looked at the boy in astonishment. How did he know what it was about? Encouraged by this sudden interest, Gerard stayed beside Mr. Simons. Now they were in the street, which was out-of-bounds during school hours. He looked around to see whether the others were watching him.

"Teacher's pet!" Piet shouted after him.

But that didn't bother Gerard. Excitedly he reported to Mr. Simons all Victor had told them.

"Well, well," Mr. Simons said slowly, as he read the notice. Gerard, too, was studying the poster, hoping to find something even Victor would not know about.

"Hadn't you better get back inside?" Mr. Simons asked abruptly.

"Oh . . . yes . . . yes, of course, sir." Gerard went back to the gate of the playground as slowly as he dared, so that the others wouldn't know he'd been sent back.

"What does it say?" the first-form boys, who had also heard Victor's story, asked Gerard inquisitively.

"Oh, nothing you need worry about," Gerard answered condescendingly.

"Mind they don't stick a 'wanted' notice up for you some day," Tim called from a distance.

"Oh I do hope they get away," Nicky said to no one in particular. But she looked directly at Matthew as she spoke.

What did she expect him to do about it?

CHAPTER FIVE

Water! Water!

"You're rather quiet today, Matthew. Did something go wrong at school? Did you get a bad mark for your homework?"

Matthew looked away. He did not want his mother to see his face.

"No, nothing much happened, really. Piet and Gerard had one of their fights. Simons nearly caught them at it." He kept his eyes glued to the windshield. Mother always drove so fast that the car simply swallowed the road, as if somewhere between its wheels was a large hole into which the road disappeared.

Had Mother heard about the runaways? She must have passed at least one of the notices, for the police had stuck them up everywhere. But then it was just like her not even to see them. Mother never paid the slightest attention to that sort of thing.

They drove in silence for a while, then Mother said, "I saw Enriqui working on your boat this morning. He seemed to be giving it a jolly good scrub."

"I never asked him to." Matthew was afraid that she might be reproaching him. Father had given him the *Eline* on the understanding that he was to look after her entirely by himself.

"I'm sure you didn't, darling." Just then a small black pig

came ambling across the narrow road, and Mother had to swerve hard. The long spines of a cactus scraped against the mudguard and doors of the car. Instinctively, Matthew drew back his head, as if he needed to protect himself against the spine outside.

"Mind the little goat, Mummy," he shouted, pointing to a kid that was half hidden from sight by the thick foliage of an agave tree. "They ought to keep their animals in," he grumbled, as the brakes squealed a second time.

"You know how hard it is for them. The natives haven't nearly enough land for their animals."

"Alfredo told me yesterday that his cousin's donkey . . . you know that cousin of his who lives in the Second District . . . well, his cousin's donkey broke loose again and the police caught it. He was told to fetch it from the station and pay a fine. If he doesn't call for it within a fortnight, the police are going to sell it. And Antonio, that's the cousin's name, says he absolutely refuses to pay up this time. The donkey keeps running off, and all Antonio ever does is pay fines for it. He says the police are even stupider than his donkey, because a donkey can't possibly know it's wrong to run away, and the police expect it to know all the same."

Mother laughed. "You hardly ever ride either of the donkeys these days, do you?" she asked, serious again.

"I like sailing the *Eline* much better."

"But why must you keep going to Hollow Tongue day after day? Couldn't you sometimes do your homework at home, as you used to before you got your boat?" Mother looked at him out of the corner of her eye.

"I bet Enriqui has been talking to you," Matthew said suspiciously. "All that nonsense about the place being haunted! Why don't you come along with me one day and see for yourself? Honestly, Hollow Tongue's just an ordinary island. Or are you afraid of it, too?"

"No, I'm not. If I get a chance I'll certainly come along to see for myself." Mother slowed down again, for they had reached the gates of Brakkeput. "I called on Aunt Else this morning," she said. "I've asked her and your uncle to bring Nicky over to spend a day with us next week." Mother was wondering how Matthew would take it. To her surprise, he merely mumbled, "Oh, well . . ." and left it at that.

"You'll simply have to take Nicky out in the boat, you know," Mother continued cautiously. "And not like last time, either . . ."

"But she won't dare to come to Hollow Tongue," Matthew broke in. "Everyone at school is afraid of the place."

"You and your stories!" Mother shook her head. Matthew could see her doing it, even though he was not looking at her.

"I'm not telling you stories. I'm simply telling the truth."

"You won't forget to change into your old trousers before you go out in your boat, will you?" Mother asked as she got out of the car.

By way of reply, Matthew bounded up the stairs and disappeared into the house. He must get away to Hollow Tongue as quickly as possible. No one would bother him on the island, and he would have a real chance to think about what the boys had said at school. He might even hit on a scheme for helping the runaways.

"Put on your old trousers, will you!" Paulina shouted, seeing that Matthew was trying to sneak out by the back door.

"You always make such a fuss!" Matthew grumbled. But he went back to change, all the same.

"Hey, you!" Paulina called as she saw him going out for the second time.

"What on earth is it now?" Matthew refused to budge. If she wanted to speak to him, let her come outside. All the same, he glanced around nervously to see if Father was about. Father had more than once told him off for being rude to Paulina.

"Psst. . . ." Paulina was beckoning to him. Reluctantly Matthew took a few steps toward her. He was balancing his satchel on his head with his right hand, as protection against the blistering sun. He stopped and waited for Paulina to come up to him.

"Enriqui . . ." she panted when she was close enough.

"I suppose Enriqui has been dreaming again," he scoffed.

Paulina shook her head, and she looked so grave that Matthew suddenly went cold all over. He had often felt like this in the days before he had first set foot on Hollow Tongue, the days when he had still believed all the rumors about the little island.

"Enriqui spotted a bird on your tent this morning . . . a pitch-black bird it was . . . its head tucked under its wings . . . that's a sure sign of sickness, that is . . . Enriqui says you mustn't go back to the island . . . not today . . . not tomorrow . . . not ever again . . . you'll be sorry if you do . . . don't go to the island, Matthew. . . ." She whispered the last words with terrible urgency.

"There are hundreds of birds on the island!" Matthew tried to sound unperturbed, but his voice gave him away. His heart was pounding now, and he had to swallow hard. "There are hundred of birds," he repeated. "They just come to hunt for food. What's so odd about that?"

"A black bird . . . its head tucked under its wings . . . stock-still on your tent. . . ." Paulina was gripping his arm.

Matthew could feel her big hot hands bruising his flesh. She was hurting him, but he did not mind, for at least she was there with him, alive and real. In Brakkeput, you often didn't know what was real and what wasn't, and you couldn't always tell whether you were awake or dreaming.

He was half inclined to follow Paulina's advice and keep away from Hollow Tongue for good. Mother would be delighted. But Father would ask questions. And if his classmates ever heard about it!

He dared not look at Paulina, for fear she might guess his thoughts. He peered across the yard from under his satchel. In the distance he could just make out the bay, but Hollow Tongue lay hidden from view.

"You're not to go, do you hear me?" Paulina insisted. That did it. If she had only kept quiet then, Matthew would probably have done as he was told. But now he pulled himself free with such a jerk that his satchel fell off his head. Snatching it up, he raced down to the beach as fast as he knew how.

The beach was quite deserted, but his boat showed clearly that someone had been working on her not so long ago. Before he pushed her into the water, Matthew took a quick look around. Everything was so terribly quiet. Now and then a gust of wind rustled the leaves, and an occasional sea gull pierced the silence with its high-pitched mew. Somehow the afternoon seemed quite different from any that had gone before.

Nonsense, Matthew tried to reassure himself. It was just Paulina's scary chatter.

Any other day he would have made straight for Hollow Tongue. But today he let the boat drift into the bay, past the little creek where Enriqui and the other natives kept their fishing gear. Not a soul was to be seen anywhere.

He tried to give himself courage by whistling a tune. But his lips were bone-dry. Licking them didn't do much good either. Perhaps if he sipped some water. . . . But the water bottle which he usually kept under the seat was not there today. Enriqui, of course, Matthew thought. Should he go back to fetch another bottle? But wasn't that just an excuse for not going on to Hollow Tongue? Once he went back, Paulina would make quite certain that he did not get away a second time. And then it would not be his fault if he gave the island a miss.

But while he was still debating the question, he had already steered the boat to Hollow Tongue. He had got to know his *Eline* so well that he could have sailed her almost in his sleep, even against the strongest gale.

Just off the island he hesitated for a moment; should he sail on or land? Before he quite knew what had happened, he had flung the rope over the rock. Automatically, he now threw the old tire over the side to save the *Eline* from being scratched. Then he lowered the sail and shipped the rudder.

From where he stood, he could just make out the top of his tent, and nothing else. But he could have sworn that a shadow had moved up there.

"The canvas must have been flapping in the wind, that's all," he told himself. He looked at his boat. There she lay, quite indifferent to anything that might be happening on the island. She had suddenly turned into a complete stranger, someone who would leave you in the lurch when you most needed help.

Matthew picked up his satchel and began to climb the rock. A few steps and he was at the top. He peered nervously all around him. Not a sign of life anywhere. And yet he had the feeling that someone was about. And very close, too. He clutched his satchel, his only weapon against sudden attack.

"Please... oh, please..." he mumbled to himself, without really knowing why. Sweat was pouring down his face. He opened his eyes so wide that they hurt. If he closed them even for a second, something terrible was sure to happen. He must keep his wits about him, or else ... or else ...

And then it happened. The tent flap moved. His gasp sounded so loud in his own ears that he thought he must have screamed very loud.

His first impulse was to race back to the boat. But his legs seemed glued to the rock. Carefully he tried to shift one, hoping that he would not make a sound. Once he found he could move it, he shifted the other leg as well. Now he was standing right in front of the tent. He would look in, yes, he would simply have to look in ... but what if the danger lay outside?

Then suddenly, right next to him, he heard a groan. As if someone were having a terrible nightmare. He dropped his satchel like a hot brick. Someone had come to Hollow Tongue; someone was in his tent.

Still, it was a person then, not a ghost! His fear was gone, even though his heart was still hammering furiously. With a sweep of his hand he pulled back the flap of the tent.

A complete stranger! There he lay, stretched out on the camp bed. He was lying on his stomach, his hands clawing the mattress, his head buried in it. But for the groan he had heard, Matthew would have thought he was dead.

It did not seem to matter right now *why* the stranger was in the tent. He was terribly ill.

Matthew leaned forward and tapped him gently on the shoulder. The man did not move. Only his back went on rising and falling, so that Matthew knew he was still alive. Matthew looked around: he had no idea what to do next. It was stifling in the tent—the sun had been beating down on it all day. Perhaps the man was dying. He must get help. But first he must open the flap wide, to let in some fresh air.

He crawled out of the tent, without taking his eyes off the man for a single moment. Perhaps he was shamming, waiting his chance to pounce the moment Matthew's back was turned.

As Matthew was rolling up the flap, he heard the man groan again. He must be thirsty, Matthew thought. And to-day of all days he had to be without water! Should he go back home to fetch some, after all? He peered toward Brakkeput. Everything looked as it had done a little while ago—quite deserted.

Suddenly Matthew had an idea. He clambered down the

rock to his boat and found a tin that Enriqui must have over-
looked. He filled the tin with sea water, then, slowly so as
not to spill any, he made his way back to the tent.

The man had not moved. Matthew put the tin down by
the bed. He tapped the man again, this time a little harder.
The groans became louder.

"Look," Matthew said in a whisper, as if he were afraid
they might be overheard. "I've brought you some water.
I'll pour it over your wrists." He lifted one of the man's
arms, and began to pour the water over it. The man's wrists
were strong and hairy, Matthew observed. His fingers were
long and thin, and calloused on the inside.

At first, Matthew had thought that the man's hands were
black. But as he went on pouring water over them, he was
surprised to see that the wrists were turning whiter and
whiter.

"If only I could get a glimpse of his face," Matthew
thought. But he could not bring himself to lift the man's
head. "He will scream if I do," Matthew tried to persuade
himself. The truth was that he was afraid.

The groaning had stopped now. Matthew looked around
the tent again, to see if there was anything else he could do
for the man. He would certainly need drinking water and
perhaps some medicine as well. If he hurried, he could be
back from Brakkeput within fifteen minutes.

He gave the man a last glance. He did not look as if he
could run away. And anyway, where could he run to? The
only house in the neighborhood was theirs.

Matthew did not know why, but he felt sure the man did

not want anyone to see him. Perhaps he had hidden his face quite deliberately.

On the way home Matthew thought about the way the man could have come to Hollow Tongue. But he still refused to admit to himself what deep down he knew to be the truth about the stranger. From his boat he looked back at Hollow Tongue. The little island seemed just the same place it had been yesterday and the day before. And yet it was no longer the same. Now it had become even more mysterious. Would other people feel it?

He would not tell anyone of his discovery before he had had a chance to talk to the stranger. And if the man refused to tell him anything . . . well, he would just have to keep quiet for good. Matthew had read that the ancients always received strangers with a great show of hospitality, and that good hosts never asked questions.

"Matthew, Matthew. . . ." Just his luck! Paulina had seen him running up from the beach. He tried to dodge behind a large tamarind, but it was too late.

"Will you come here at once!" She had just chased a stray turkey from the yard with a broomstick, and now she was waving the stick at Matthew.

Just pretend nothing has happened, Matthew told himself. He pulled the kind of innocent face that old Joseph always pulled when Father gave him a scolding, and came out from behind the tree.

"I forgot to take water," he shouted as he tried to slip past Paulina into the kitchen.

"Don't you take any of my water!" Paulina shouted back

at him. "We haven't nearly enough and I've still half the cooking to do!"

But Matthew had already opened the refrigerator and taken out one of the bottles.

"Perhaps it will rain," he teased as he raced out of the other kitchen door. Paulina's shouts followed him a long way.

She certainly had every right to be cross, he admitted to himself. In Brakkeput, you couldn't just turn on a tap every time you wanted water. First the water had to be pumped into the storage tank. Then it had to be boiled, filtered, refiltered, and finally cooled in the refrigerator. It was a long-drawn-out business, and it always put Paulina in a very bad temper. To her all these precautions were just so much stuff and nonsense. Now the tank was probably almost empty again, and Joseph had a trick of disappearing whenever it came to pumping. Still Enriqui was sure to be close at hand, and he would help her.

Paulina was now calling Joseph at the top of her voice, her shrieks reverberating through the entire plantation. Matthew could still hear her down in the bay, as he jumped into the boat and pushed off.

On Hollow Tongue only the tent could be seen, nothing else.

Then, quite suddenly, Paulina's black bird was hovering over the tent. Matthew felt his stomach turn over. That black bird again! How did the bird know that a man lay sick on the island?

CHAPTER SIX

Help Comes at Night

"It's getting pretty dark outside," Matthew said, turning his head and looking through the tent flap. Twilight on the island never lasted for more than a quarter of an hour, and he had to be home before dark.

Matthew had been sitting by the man for over an hour. He had given him water, he had given him fruit, but he had never yet dared to look him straight in the face.

For one thing, his own glances always seemed to be evaded. At first Matthew had been rather hurt by this, then it occurred to him that perhaps the man was still afraid of being given away, in spite of everything. But, if the man was afraid of being betrayed, Matthew thought, perhaps he was a real criminal after all.

But he hid his curiosity and his fears, for there were more urgent things to think about. Whoever the man was, Matthew realized that if he spent the night on the rock he would be dead by morning. He was shaking with fever, and once the sun was gone, it would become cold on the island.

"It just can't be done," Matthew said, thinking aloud to make the silence less oppressive. Silence can seem more oppressive when you are with someone else than when you are alone. So he kept on talking aloud to himself. "I must try to smuggle a blanket out of the house." But that was easier said than done. "What an idiot I was not to have thought of that

before. I should have realized he'd have to spend at least
one night here."

The stranger remained silent, and Matthew continued to
make his plans. "A blanket and a few aspirins," he repeated
under his breath. "And as much food as possible. Pity it isn't
Paulina's night out." Then he stopped short. Even if he
could get hold of all these things and get them out of the
house without being seen, how would he get back to Hollow
Tongue? He wasn't supposed to take his boat out after dark.

"Too bad," Matthew said to himself right out loud. Nobody had actually forbidden him to sail at night. It was just
taken for granted that he would not do it. He'd have to
chance it, go to bed as usual, and slip out half an hour or so
later. With a bit of luck, no one would ever get to know
about it. The man would just have to make do without a
blanket for a few hours.

"I have to go," Matthew told the man on the mattress, still not looking at him. A movement which he felt rather than saw seemed to be some sort of reply.

He probably doesn't understand a word I say, Matthew thought. He pushed the box he had been sitting on into the corner of the tent, so that the man wouldn't trip over it if he got up. If he's one of those men from Uquique, went on Matthew to himself, he probably only speaks Spanish and a bit of English.

As he bent down to crawl out of the tent, Matthew saw a big shadow over his head. The black bird! It was Enriqui's black bird again for the second time today. Yet before today he'd never seen it on Hollow Tongue.

Matthew backed quickly into the safety of the tent again. Far better spend the night in the company of the dying man, than sail all by himself across the silent bay, with this sinister bird as his only companion.

Suddenly the man spoke for the first time. "*Aqua*," he whispered. Happy to hear him speak at last, Matthew groped for the water bottle. He had put it outside ready to take home for refilling, but it wasn't quite empty. Carefully, he poured the last few drops into a plastic beaker, then knelt down and held it out to the stranger. Best see if he could drink by himself. But the stranger was obviously still much too weak. He stretched out his hand, but that was all he could manage. Gently Matthew pushed his hand under the man's neck and raised his head. Then he poured the water slowly into the man's open mouth. Most of it ran down his chin.

"*Dioso*," Matthew swore. It was what Joseph always said when things went wrong, but perhaps coming from him it sounded odd, because the man grinned. Matthew went scarlet. And at that moment, he made up his mind that whatever happened he would not let this man down. For anyone who could look so friendly couldn't possibly have anything very terrible on his conscience.

Perhaps the man guessed what he was thinking, for he seized Matthew's hand and held it so tight that Matthew dropped the beaker and almost cried out.

"If he can grip like that when he's sick, he must be mighty tough when he's fit." For a moment, Matthew was afraid of him again. But he fought the feeling down.

A man, a sick man, was lying here, on his island. His only job was to see to it that the man got better. Everything else would have to wait.

Matthew lay in bed listening to the insects buzzing outside his mosquito net. Normally he hardly noticed them, but tonight they sounded different. It was almost as if they knew what he was going to do, and were saying urgently: don't do it, don't do it, don't do it.

I must wait a little longer, Matthew thought, and tried to think about something else. He remembered that he hadn't quite finished his homework because he had stayed on Hollow Tongue too long.

Father had said something about it at dinner, although that was probably because he had been in a bad temper. Joseph and Alfredo had just told him that they had to go to a family feast in Santa Cruz next week. "The two of them have made the whole thing up, of course," Father had said crossly, when he was telling Mother about it. "But it's no use my saying no, because they'll go for good if I make difficulties, and you know what it's like these days trying to get anyone to work on a plantation! We've worked here all our lives and built the country up, and then those chaps at the refinery come along and take the whole place over, and our needs are ignored. It's a disgrace. Of course the hands won't work on the land when they can get higher wages in the refinery."

"Oh, I don't know," Mother said, "what about people like Enriqui?"

"Enriqui's different, of course, but they don't come like that nowadays. He's earned his retirement, and he ought to be taking things easy now."

"But Enriqui told me himself that he'd much rather work than sit about doing nothing all day," Matthew said. He guessed why Alfredo and Joseph had suddenly decided they must go away. It was all because of the black bird. In Santa Cruz they had an aunt who knew all about magic, or *broeha* as they called it. No doubt she would have a potion to save them from the danger foretold by the black bird. But if he told Father that, he would get even crosser. So Matthew had decided to say nothing.

Matthew caught himself yawning. He must be careful not to fall asleep. If the stranger were left on Hollow Tongue without a blanket all night, his fever would get worse, and he might even die!

At this Matthew sat up with a jerk. How would he explain that he couldn't go back to a dead man on the island? He'd have to say that Enriqui and the others were right after all, there was a hoodoo on Hollow Tongue. The thought of never returning to Hollow Tongue made him sigh with relief. But then he remembered that the stranger was still alive and needed him.

That afternoon, the whole thing had seemed a tremendous adventure, the kind you read about in books. But now he was actually involved in it there was no time to enjoy it, or to think about how exciting it all was.

He looked at the provisions arranged around his bed. "Aspirins, bread, bananas, papaw, and a smoked sausage. Tomorrow, the minute school's over, I must buy another sausage and a new bottle of aspirins. I only hope Paulina won't have noticed that all this stuff is missing. And if my pocket money isn't enough, I'll have to ask Piet to help me out." Of course, he wouldn't be able to tell Piet what the money was for. No one, no one at all, must have the slightest inkling that there was a man on Hollow Tongue. The stranger had gripped his hand, and Matthew felt they were bound together.

I wonder if one blanket will be enough, Matthew thought. It would just have to be, for he daren't take more than one. Mother was so fussy about her linen cupboard. If she looked inside, she'd see at once that there was a blanket missing, and she'd probably suspect Joseph or Alfredo.

Matthew suddenly felt depressed again, and gulped some water to try to settle the lump in his throat. Then, carefully, he slipped off the bed. He groped for the flap in the mosquito net, and felt for the water bottle. "Now the beaker. Where on earth did I put it? Ah, here it is. No, it's the papaw." He pushed it aside, then gasped as something suddenly fell over. The noise wasn't much, but coming unexpectedly, it made him go cold all over. At that instant, he wanted to creep back into bed, go to sleep, and wake up the next morning to find that the whole adventure had been a bad dream—that there had never been a sick stranger in his tent on Hollow Tongue, and that the sinister black bird had never appeared in the bay. But it wasn't a dream, the stranger was real, and Matthew had pledged himself to help him.

He packed all the provisions carefully into a bag, put the water bottle and the beaker on top and the blanket over his arm. He was just tiptoeing out when he realized that he was still wearing pajamas. Impatient at his own stupidity, he dressed quickly, checked to see if his torch was working, picked up his load again, and prepared to set off.

Apart from the radio, the house was silent. Once he was across the patio and the yard, the rest would be easy. "Do everything just as usual, don't try to be too careful . . ." he kept telling himself. If you took too many precautions, something always went wrong.

He had reached the bottom of the stairs now, and he stopped to make sure that his parents had not heard him. He waited a little longer, in case Paulina was about, then "Now!" he said to himself, and was across the patio and the yard without really knowing how he had got there so quickly.

Out on the plantation it was much darker than he had expected, but he was reassured by the familiar creaking sound of the windmills. He knew the way to the bay so well that he could find it even in the dark. Remembering the hornets, he gave the mangrove bush a wide berth, and made for the beach to find the *Eline* looking like a wreck in the strange shadows cast by the bright moonlight. Matthew could not get rid of the feeling that he was being watched. He bent down as he ran toward the boat, and stopped several times to look back toward the bushes, afraid that someone might be lurking there. It was just the sort of place where the black bird might go to roost, if it ever went to sleep at all.

"Well, now for Hollow Tongue," Matthew said softly to his boat to calm himself. "Let's see what's going on there. I hope the man won't get a fright when he hears me coming. I'd better whistle softly before we land. . . ." Gently, he pushed the *Eline* into the water. Before getting in, he took a last long look at the plantation. For all he knew he might never see it again! He was the first person ever to sail in the bay at night. The natives told so many stories . . . what if there really were something in them. . . .

"Nothing at all can happen," he said, speaking to the *Eline* again, as he steered skillfully in the direction of Hollow Tongue. "After all, if no one has ever been out in the bay after dark before, how can they possibly know what goes on here at night? Enriqui's just talking rubbish. He's getting old, Father said so at dinner tonight. And old people always get things mixed up. Half the time they don't know what they're saying."

There was no answer from the *Eline*, and Matthew squeezed the tiller harder, as if that would make her reply.

"We won't stay out long. We'll just land, see how he's doing, give him some water and a few aspirins, and then straight back home," he said persuasively.

But the *Eline* kept silent, and he felt as if she were trying to escape from his hands.

"I wonder if the wind changes at night?" Matthew looked at the pennant. He was now close to Hollow Tongue. If he came about too quickly, he would be dashed against the rocks. The far side of the island was in shadow.

The *Eline* veered much too far to the right, and Matthew became so absorbed in the task of bringing the boat in that he almost forgot the purpose of his visit.

"There we are!" he said triumphantly to the *Eline*, when she was safely moored. "Lie still till I get back!" Once he had said it, he remembered Enriqui's story that boats had a mysterious habit of disappearing in Big Mouth.

Carrying his bag of provisions and the blanket, he crept toward the tent. Not a sound! The stranger must be asleep. Or unconscious perhaps.

Carefully Matthew lifted the tent flap. He switched on his torch. The tent was empty!

Then he felt a hand on his shoulder, and his heart missed a beat. He did not dare look around. He all but screamed. The hand pushed him into the tent, and then released him.

He heard a chuckle. Matthew looked around then, straight into the stranger's face. The man must have been hiding behind the tent while Matthew was tying up the *Eline*. Of course, he was afraid of intruders. Who wouldn't be, in his place? Matthew too began to laugh, and he picked up the bag and the blanket to show the man why he had come. "Ah . . ." said the man.

A shaft of moonlight shone into the tent through the open flap. Matthew unpacked his bag, put all its contents on the wooden box, and threw the blanket down on the bed.

All this time, although the stranger was watching him closely, Matthew kept silent. If only he would say something, I'd at least know what language he speaks, Matthew thought. The man still said nothing. Matthew reached for the aspirins. How could he explain what they were for? "These are for your fever," he said, speaking very slowly, and he handed the bottle to the stranger, who looked at it carefully, then took it in his hand, and turned it over and over, inspecting it from all sides.

I suppose he's better, Matthew thought. Perhaps he's wondering whether to take them or not.

"I'll be back tomorrow. I live over there." He pointed in the direction of Brakkeput. "And my name is Matthew. Matthew van Rooy."

"Matthew . . ." the man repeated after him.

Clearly, he had understood, but from the way he said "Matthew," it was obvious that he spoke another language, not Dutch, Matthew's own.

"Good-by, then, and sleep well," Matthew said as he ducked out of the tent.

The return journey held no terrors for him now. All he was worried about was how to get back into the house undetected. Quickly he slipped down the rocks to the *Eline,* jumped in, cast off and set course for the plantation.

He had just beached the boat safely, and was taking a last look back to make quite sure that Hollow Tongue looked the same as usual, and that there was nothing to show that a man was hiding there, when he heard a noise in the mangrove bushes. Quick as lightning, he hid behind the boat.

Someone was running heavily down the path to the beach. Father?

Carefully, Matthew crept to the stern of the boat, and peeped around it.

It was Enriqui.

What on earth was he doing? Had he found out, or was he just keeping watch? Now he was taking something out of his bag and throwing it far out into the bay with a broad sweep of his arm. He must be trying to charm away the evil spirits.

Matthew nearly laughed aloud. Enriqui's "ghost" was just a man like any other, only he happened to be on the run. As soon as Enriqui was out of sight, running by the water's edge toward his hut, Matthew slipped from behind the boat into the bushes, and ran for home.

He slipped into the house without meeting anyone, and

it wasn't until he was comfortably settled in bed, still breath-less, that he suddenly remembered that he had forgotten to ask the stranger where he came from.

CHAPTER SEVEN

The Stranger and the Boat

Matthew had never slept so badly in his life. Several times he woke in terror. Once, he thought the black bird was flying toward him. Another time he felt a hand grip his neck from behind, just as the stranger's had done on Hollow Tongue. He must have screamed, that time, for his mother got out of bed and shook him gently.

"Whatever is the matter with you?" she asked anxiously, smoothing the damp hair from his forehead.

"Nothing," Matthew said, as casually as he could, and quickly pulled the sheet over his face, afraid that his expression might give him away.

Mother pulled the sheet down again. "That won't help you to sleep. You must have plenty of air. And you must lie on your side. Then you won't have nightmares."

Obediently, Matthew turned on his side, his face to the wall, and pretended to be asleep. As long as Mother was satisfied that it was only lying on his back that had given him nightmares, his secret was safe.

Next morning he was up early. Paulina wasn't in yet, so he knew it was not yet half-past five. Like Alfredo, Joseph and Enriqui, she lived near the creek, and she was very proud of her little house.

"My house is the prettiest of the lot," she always said. Actually, from the outside hers looked just like all the others.

77

It was the inside she was so proud of, for it was furnished with things given her by Matthew's parents, a table and some chairs, an old-fashioned gramophone, and a chest of drawers adorned with an assortment of photographs, mostly of Matthew. Matthew used to like going to Paulina's house, but lately he had begun to find her chatter embarrassing. She never talked about anything but his family—what a sweet little boy he had been, what saints his father and mother were—until Matthew didn't know which way to look. And it was so hard not to laugh when Paulina called his father "a real lady"—an expression the natives used for men and women alike.

"I wonder if the man managed to get any sleep?" Matthew looked at his watch. It was just after five now. He didn't have to leave for school until half-past seven, so there was just time to sail to Hollow Tongue and see what was going on there.

Quietly he got up, collected his clothes, and crept into the bathroom. But mother had heard him.

"Matthew, go back to bed, it's much too early to get up."

"I only want to go for a little spin in the boat," he called back.

"You've had so little sleep. . . ." He did not hear what else Mother said, for he'd turned on the shower. He shivered under the cold water.

When he had finished, and was going downstairs, Mother called after him; "Back at quarter-past seven, do you hear?"

"Right-ho!" he said.

Downstairs, outside the larder, he hesitated, wondering

what else he could take to his friend without anyone noticing. Bananas would be all right, because nobody minded
how many of those he ate, so Mother wouldn't miss them.
And another bottle of water couldn't do any harm. Oh, and
the man would probably want a smoke.

Matthew decided to take just two cigarettes and a box of
matches from the kitchen. If he took more, their disappearance might be spotted and awkward questions asked.

"I'll pay it all back out of my pocket money," he promised
himself, as he ran through the plantation to the bay.

Thank goodness, the black bird was nowhere to be seen.
If the natives were right and it really was an ill omen, perhaps its absence this morning meant that the stranger was
better.

I'll just go out as far as the mouth of the bay and come
back again, Matthew thought. If the stranger was still asleep,
he didn't want to disturb him. The *Eline* responded so well
that Matthew had left the bay behind before he knew where
he was. "We'd better sail on a bit," he said aloud.

Then he heard someone calling his name. He looked
around and there were Enriqui, Alfredo and Joseph by the
creek, gesturing to him to come back. Crossly Matthew
swung the tiller over. He didn't know what to do. If he
sailed back along the creek, Enriqui would almost certainly
ask him why he was out sailing at this hour of the morning.
But if he just ignored them and sailed on, they'd be even
more suspicious. The best thing was to try to find out what
the three of them were up to so early. If they were going

fishing, he'd just have to wait until they were out of the bay.

"Hallo!" he called, when he was close enough for them to hear him. "Are you going fishing?"

"D'you want to come along?" Alfredo asked.

"I've got a boat of my own, now, and you know how Paulina carries on if I come home smelling of fish."

The men laughed.

"Are you allowed out so early?" Enriqui gave him a long, searching look.

"Mother knows all about it," Matthew replied and looked straight back at the old man, pretending he didn't feel at all uncomfortable. "When are you leaving?" he asked quickly.

"Right now. We're all set," said Joseph.

"I thought you were supposed to be at a family feast?" Matthew teased him, remembering. It was nice to have something to tease *them* about, for a change.

"All in good time," Alfredo replied slyly. He nudged Joseph, and gave him a meaningful wink.

Then Enriqui said something to them that Matthew could not understand. At once the two of them sprang into action and Matthew just managed to get the *Eline* out of the way before they pushed the fishing boats into the water with a lot of noise and bustle. Matthew waited until the fishing boats had got under way before he set course again for Hollow Tongue. Even so, he kept looking around to see how far the others had got, before he made straight for his island.

Matthew took his time making the *Eline* fast and whistled

loudly, so that the man shouldn't be startled when he appeared.

"Hallo there!" Matthew called out softly as he crawled into the tent.

"Hallo!" The man sat straight up on the mattress with his hair all over the place and opened his mouth in an enormous yawn.

Matthew laughed. "Sleep well?" he asked, still a little embarrassed. Even in the shade of the tent the man looked much cleaner than he had the day before. He'd probably taken a dip in the bay. Bother it, I forgot to bring any soap, Matthew thought. He ought to make a shopping list; otherwise he'd forget half the things the man needed.

He pulled out the two cigarettes and the matches from his pocket and put them down by the man's side. Then he placed the bananas and the water bottle on the box. He noticed that there was nothing left of the food and water he had brought the night before.

"Good boy," the man said in English after he had lit one of Matthew's cigarettes. Matthew blushed with pleasure because he knew enough English to realize that the man was praising him.

"When I come back from school, I'll bring you some more," Matthew said quickly, but his English wasn't good enough for that, so he said it in Dutch, hoping the man could understand.

"Some more . . . *Nog meer.* . . ." The man repeated the Dutch words. Matthew looked at him respectfully. So, he really could speak Matthew's language as well!

"I . . ." the man pointed at himself, "sailor."

Matthew nodded. Of course, in that case the man must have been all over the place. That's how he'd learned a bit of Dutch. That must be it.

"Are you still sick? Ill?" Matthew asked.

The man took a long pull at his cigarette, and shook his head.

I'd better keep quiet for a bit, Matthew thought and sat down next to the man on the ground. He still felt a little awkward sitting there in silence with a strange grownup, and didn't quite know what to do. So he just waited, occasionally picking up a crab that had wandered in and throwing it outside through the flap of the tent.

When the man had half finished his cigarette, he put it out and carefully preserved the stub. All you could hear was the sound of the birds singing on the plantation and the windmills creaking in the distance.

When the silence grew too oppressive, Matthew said; "Over there is White Bay, and there's my father's plantation, Brakkeput."

"Island?" the man asked.

"Oh, the island? It's called Curaçao."

The man nodded thoughtfully.

Taking his bearings, Matthew thought. I wonder where he's hoping to get to. He looked at the man out of the corner of his eye. There was no doubt, he had a nice, friendly face, but even so you could see that he must have gone through a lot. He looked dead tired.

Matthew didn't really mind the man speaking so little.

After all, smiles and gestures meant something too, and it was difficult to talk when you didn't know the other person's language. He looked at the stranger's hands and remembered his dream that they were choking him. They were sensitive and well-kept, not a criminal's hands at all.

"What's your name?" Matthew asked and could have bitten his tongue out as soon as he had said it. How could he have been such an idiot? The man's face was already darkening with suspicion. If he was one of the fugitives from Uquique, the last thing he would want to do was tell anyone his name!

"I shan't tell a soul," Matthew said, and to make quite clear what he meant, he put a finger to his lips.

The only reply was a few short phrases in Spanish which Matthew couldn't understand. But at least the man looked friendly again.

"Well, I must go now. I'll see you this afternoon, when I get out of school."

Matthew didn't sail straight for home. He had a lot to think about. Should he tell his parents that there was a stranger on Hollow Tongue? No, that was out of the question. He had promised to keep silent. But in that case, what could he usefully do for the stranger? Of course, he could see that he had enough food and drink and that he remained undiscovered, but clearly the man could not stay on Hollow Tongue forever.

The thought haunted Matthew, and he was silent all through breakfast, and all the way to school. Only when Piet, Tim and Victor rushed up to him and shouted all at once, "Have you heard?" did he seem to come back to earth.

"They came past yesterday at about three o'clock!" Victor was still quite out of breath from running.

"And there were only four men in the boat."

"The fifth got drowned," Tim said.

"No, he died in the boat and was thrown overboard," said Piet.

"How do you know all that?" Matthew asked. He must be careful not to ask too many questions, or the others might get suspicious.

"Get Victor to tell you, he knows most about it," Nicky said. The girls had joined the group, and the excited chatter had grown still louder.

"Well . . ." Victor paused until the others had stopped talking. "The coast guard on the Black Mountain saw a little boat floundering aimlessly in the sea. He reported it to the harbor master and to the police. . ."

"Did they catch them?" Matthew was too worried to wait for the end of the story.

"Oh, don't be such an ass," Victor said crossly.

"Why don't you let him tell it in his own way?" Mady asked.

"Dr. Van Boom, who checks all incoming ships, went out to them on the pilot boat with food, medicines and drinking water. He intercepted the boat, told the men which way to go, and then gave them all the provisions he had with him. He said that anyone who managed to get away from Uquique deserved to go free. And my father said that the men were put in prison because they were against the dictator."

"Oh, good old Dr. Van Boom!" Matthew said enthusiastically.

"And of course, once the boat was out of sight, there was precious little my father could do about it," Victor went on, with a wink.

Everyone laughed except Gerard de Wit.

"Trust the police not to risk getting hurt," he said. "You don't suppose that'll be the end of it, do you? Your father will get into trouble all right for letting five criminals escape like that!"

"Oh, you make me sick," Nicky said disgustedly.

"It was Dr. Van Boom's idea," Piet snapped at him. "It had nothing to do with Victor's father!"

"Listen, Victor!" Matthew had to shout to make himself heard above the noise. "Did Dr. Van Boom say how the men were?"

"Wretched, of course," Victor replied, "but they were terribly grateful for his help."

"He ought to be grateful they didn't do him in! Dirty criminals!" said Gerard de Wit, goading them.

Before anyone knew what had happened, Matthew had sent Gerard reeling with a punch to the jaw. "Just let me hear you say that again, if you dare! Just you try. . . !" he bellowed furiously.

"Oh, for goodness' sake, cut it out," Nicky called. "If they catch you . . ." She couldn't understand what all the fuss was about.

"They're not criminals, I tell you!" Matthew screamed. "You know as well as we do that in Uquique they throw people into jail for no reason at all. You don't have to be a criminal to get put behind bars, it's enough just to be against the government!"

"And that's a fact!" Victor added for emphasis. "They're simply political refugees! Why do you think my father let them go?"

After his outburst, Matthew knew he mustn't seem too curious. But there was one question he simply had to ask. So, as casually as he could, he said to Victor, "But what about the fifth man?"

Victor shrugged his shoulders. "Well, the posters say five men escaped, but Dr. Van Boom swears there were only four in the boat. In the town they say that the fifth man must either have been washed overboard, or else that he died of exposure and his friends had to throw him overboard, anyway."

The group fell silent, and the silence weighed Matthew down, for now there could no longer be any doubt who the stranger was. I wish he'd stayed with the others, he thought. It would have saved me a lot of bother. As it is, I have to worry all the time about him.

During the lunch hour, when he went to Piet's house to eat his sandwiches, he would have to pretend that he had to do some shopping for his mother. He sighed.

"Wake up, the bell's gone!" Nicky nudged him, and as they walked into school side by side, she whispered, "Wasn't Dr. Van Boom great? Now you don't need to . . ."

"Sh-hhh," Matthew said anxiously, looking around to
see if anyone else had heard her. He had the feeling that if

anyone so much as thought of Hollow Tongue, his secret would be out.

"We're coming to Brakkeput on Sunday. Will you take me sailing?" Nicky asked before she went to her seat. Matthew nodded, but even as he did so, he realized that it would be impossible. She might get it into her head to go to Hollow Tongue, and then he would really be sunk. He spent the whole morning wondering how he could put her off, and during the last lesson he was given lines because after three warnings his attention was still wandering.

And there was worse to come. When he got home that afternoon, he could hear Paulina going for Enriqui hammer and tongs.

"The dirty thieves. . . !" she screamed, among other insults. "And then to run away, saying they are going to a family feast! I suppose they were afraid they wouldn't get enough to eat there, so they have to pinch the last bit of sausage from the larder."

Clasping his satchel tight to his body, Matthew stopped to listen. His legs refused to carry him any farther. He had the feeling that the sausage he had bought during the lunch hour, to replace the one he had taken, showed right through his satchel. He stayed where he was, staring at the larder door. He must get in without Paulina noticing! But the door always squeaked, and for a few seconds he felt it just couldn't be done.

Luckily, Father and Mother were still in the living room. He hoped fervently that they hadn't noticed there were some cigarettes missing. He'd have to put those back later, but for the moment Paulina was the problem.

He reached the larder door in a couple of long strides, and slipped inside, looking fearfully up at the ceiling in case there were cockroaches.

"Done it!" The sausage was in its place, and he was out again so quickly that he could still hear Paulina raging.

"What on earth's the matter with you?" he asked innocently as he stepped into the kitchen. He winked at Enriqui behind Paulina's broad back, but there was no answering wink, so there must be something upsetting him too.

And then Paulina told her tale of the wickedness of Joseph and Alfredo, who had stolen a whole two-pound sausage.

"Are you sure you've had a proper look?" Matthew said. It was not a very tactful thing to say. Paulina knew she wasn't getting any younger, but she resented being reminded of it by other people, and she got crosser than ever.

"Perhaps the black bird has made off with your sausage," Matthew said, but his attempt at humor fell flat. Enriqui scowled, and Paulina stalked angrily out of the kitchen toward the larder. He ran after her, for he didn't want to stay with Enriqui. For all he knew, Enriqui might have seen him last night, hiding behind the *Eline*.

He heard Paulina's gasp of astonishment as she came upon the sausage. "What did I tell you!" Matthew said. If she had gone on accusing Alfredo and Joseph, and told Mother, there would have been trouble. The trickiest part had gone off very well. Now all he had to do was return the cigarettes. That was simple.

Everyone had got so used to Matthew dashing off to Hollow Tongue straight after lunch that he had no trouble getting away. And although this time he was expecting it, it was still a bit of a shock to see the stranger sitting in his tent, his legs pulled up on the mattress, and his head resting on his knees. Just as if it weren't my tent any more, Matthew thought. Now he could no longer lounge about doing his homework, for the man would be watching him all the time.

"Hallo," Matthew said, and arranged his purchases on the mattress, cigarettes on top.

The man was looking in Matthew's direction, but Matthew got the impression that he wasn't seeing anything. So he pointed first at his purchases and then at the stranger, saying as he did so, "These are for you."

The man picked up the packet of cigarettes and kept turning it in his hand, looking at it so intently that Matthew became curious. What was so odd about it? They were ordinary cigarettes, the kind his father always smoked. He had bought them, and taken out two to replace the ones he'd taken yesterday. Was the man offended at being offered an opened packet?

No, he was looking at the outside. Matthew crept a little closer, on the pretext of arranging his school books before he started his homework, so that he could get a good look at the cigarette packet himself.

And then he realized what it was that was holding the stranger's gaze. The packet was decorated with a large colored picture of a sailing boat. Did it remind him of the

boat in which he had escaped? Of his friends . . . and what
had happened? Or . . .

Matthew dared not think further. He crawled out of the
tent. The *Eline* was still there. She was the first thing he
saw when he got outside, but he tried not to look at her in
case the stranger somehow sensed what he was thinking.
No, he thought desperately, no, not the *Eline*.

He glanced back at the tent to make sure the man wasn't
watching, then looked across the bay to where he beached
his boat, trying to estimate how far it was. Not far enough.
Anyone could swim it easily. And you couldn't put a lock
on a boat.

He'd tell the man the bay was infested with sharks! No,
that was no good. He'd probably had to swim quite a distance to get to Hollow Tongue in the first place, so he would
know that wasn't true.

Matthew clenched his fists. I was *helping*! he thought.
Why has it all stopped being so simple?

CHAPTER EIGHT

Nearly Wrecked

Nicky had come. "I've brought my swimsuit," was the first thing she said. "So that we can go sailing...."

"We'll go out later," Matthew told her quickly.

"Aren't you going to say hallo to Aunt Else and Uncle Dick?" his father asked.

Matthew shook hands, scowling. He didn't care for visitors. Usually when his parents had guests he kept well out of the way. But today was different. The longer he stayed to talk, the longer he'd be able to keep Nicky away from Hollow Tongue.

So he sat quietly sipping his lemonade, and trying to act the perfect gentleman. He was so successful that once when he caught sight of his reflection in a mirror he almost burst out laughing. He looked like a boy in an advertisement, sitting there with his head on one side, listening politely to the grownups talking.

He pretended not to see his mother's surprised glances in his direction, as she wondered why he was still indoors, or Nicky's secret signals that they ought to slip away.

But being ignored didn't suit Nicky. She suddenly interrupted the conversation to say, "What a wet blanket you are today, Matthew."

"Nicky!" said her mother. But everybody was looking

at Matthew, and he realized he couldn't stay where he was any longer without making people suspicious.

"All right, then," he said ungraciously, and sighed so heavily that his father burst out laughing.

"Another few years, and he won't be so unwilling to take a girl out sailing," said Uncle Dick, chuckling.

Very funny! Matthew thought, reluctantly following Nicky out of the room.

"Look, Matthew . . ." Nicky began, hesitantly, as soon as they were outside.

"Now what?"

"If you'd rather not . . . we could quite easily just go swimming. . . ." She didn't look at him as she spoke, and Matthew felt a beast. He knew Nicky had been looking forward to going sailing with him, and now, just because she could see Matthew did not want to take her, she was saying it didn't matter.

He swallowed hard. After all, Nicky was his cousin, even if she was a girl.

"Oh, it's all right," he said ungraciously at last. "I don't mind. I'll teach you to sail if you like." Her face lit up and he thought, If I let her sail the *Eline* herself, perhaps she won't think of asking to go to the island. Without waiting for her to speak, he turned and ran back to the house, shouting over his shoulder that he was just going to change.

Through the shutters he could see Nicky standing in the patio.

I hope everything goes off all right, he thought. As long

as the man stays in the tent, as I told him to do, she won't notice anything unusual.

And in fact everything seemed to go very smoothly indeed. Nicky was kept so busy trying to follow Matthew's instructions that she hardly had time to speak, and Matthew saw to it that they kept well away from Hollow Tongue.

When, toward lunchtime, Matthew let her take the tiller, she asked him timidly, "Do you think I'm doing all right?"

"Not bad at all," Matthew said generously, "in fact, for a beginner you're really very good." But he brought the boat in himself, just the same. There were tricky currents in the bay, and though he never had any trouble himself coming in, he didn't want to run any risks with a novice in charge.

"We haven't been in the water once," Nicky said, when she'd helped Matthew to pull the dinghy up on the beach. "Couldn't we have a swim now?"

Matthew looked at his watch. "We've still a quarter of an hour to spare."

Nicky was first in the water. She dived under, and Matthew waited for her to come up. Nicky was a better swimmer than he, and could stay under much longer.

There she was at last, but she was much farther out than he'd expected. "Nicky!" Matthew shouted to her. "Not so far out!" She shouted something in reply, but he couldn't make out what. He went in after her, swimming faster than he had ever done before. He had to stop her! When he finally caught her up he was so out of breath he could hardly speak.

"What's the matter?" she asked in surprise. She was float-
ing on her back, and trying to splash him with her feet.

"Mother doesn't like me to come so far out. You can
never tell with the sharks. . . ."

Nicky at once turned over and started for the shore. She
was terrified, and oddly her terror infected Matthew, even
though he knew that there were no sharks about, and that
he had simply invented them to keep her away from Hollow
Tongue.

"Let's go back then," she said. "Pity, really. We were
only a few yards from Hollow Tongue."

"Is that where you wanted to go? You must be mad."
Matthew said sharply. And he threw a sidelong glance at
the island, to make sure the man was keeping under cover.

"Well, you go there every day," Nicky said.

"Not any more." Matthew hoped she'd believe him. As
they scrambled up the beach, he enlarged. "Enriqui has
been making such an awful fuss. A little while ago he saw a
bad man in one of his dreams, and several times last week a
black bird flew over Hollow Tongue. It perched on my
tent. I saw it myself as I sailed away from the island."

Nicky looked back at the mysterious island. "And did
you go back even after that?"

"Of course I did," Matthew couldn't help saying
proudly. Nicky stared, and he realized his mistake.

"But really, of course, I was scared to death," he added
hastily.

Nicky laughed. Just like Matthew to say that. Piet and
Tim would have bitten their tongues off rather than admit

there was something they were afraid of. But when it came to the point they were probably much more frightened than Matthew.

"There goes the gong. Lunchtime!" Matthew gave Nicky a shove and ran off. She tore after him, and chased him right across the plantation to the house.

"Calm down," Aunt Else called as she saw them racing across the patio.

"I can sail all by myself, Mummy. Matthew says I'm doing marvelously." Nicky chortled with joy.

"Go and change quickly. You too, Matthew," his mother said.

"Hollow Tongue this afternoon!" Nicky shouted to Matthew as she went upstairs.

"Not if I know it," Matthew muttered to himself.

"Just you be careful with your silly nonsense," Paulina, who had overheard them, said to Nicky. "The black bird..." She shuffled on and the rest of her sentence was lost.

"I don't give two hoots for your black birds!" Nicky called after her.

But when they went down to the beach after lunch, Matthew realized that her courage had evaporated, and it was safe to taunt her a bit. She had given him quite a scare, swimming almost out to Hollow Tongue, and he wanted to get his own back.

"Well, do you want to go to Hollow Tongue, or not?" he asked.

"Are you going?"

"I'm asking you."

"If you're not going yourself . . ." Nicky was drawing something in the sand with her foot. Matthew looked at it. It looked very much like a bird. When Nicky saw him watching, she quickly rubbed it out.

"I've got a much better idea," she said. "We'll take it in turns to sail the boat, and the one who's not sailing can hang on to a rope behind and be pulled through the bay."

"Suits me," Matthew replied, only too happy to fall in with any plan which did not include Hollow Tongue.

But he regretted it as soon as the line was in the water. He must have been mad to think of leaving Nicky alone in the boat when she'd never sailed until this morning. If anything went wrong he would be dangling on the end of a rope, and quite unable to help.

"You first," Nicky said, tying Matthew's spare rope to the cleat.

"That's no way to tie a rope," Matthew told her as he saw her fumbling with the knot. "Give it to me." He tied the rope and threw it to his cousin. "When you get tired just give me a shout." He jumped into the boat, while Nicky waded into the water.

"Don't go too far out, will you?" Nicky called.

Everything went well until Nicky decided she had had enough and that it was her turn to do some sailing. Matthew tried to talk her out of it.

"You're much too tired," he said, "and you wouldn't know what to do if we met another boat. Thank you very much, but . . ."

"Oh, stop fussing!" Nicky, who had meanwhile climbed

aboard, pushed Matthew so hard that he lost his balance.
She quickly seized the opportunity to snatch the tiller from
his grasp, and the *Eline* lurched. Matthew sat down with a
bump.

"You couldn't really have thought I'd leave you in
charge," he said. But when Nicky had sailed the *Eline* safely
and skillfully around the bay for a quarter of an hour, he
began to feel it was cheating not to let her try on her own.
After all, he had promised, and it wasn't as if he was afraid
she might make for Hollow Tongue. The story about the
black bird seemed to have settled that. He glanced around
quickly to make sure everything was in order. "Carry on,
skipper," he said.

Nicky was in such a hurry to get him overboard, in case
he changed his mind at the last moment, that she almost
threw him out, bracing herself so as not to overbalance when
he went over the side. But Matthew slid into the water so
carefully that there was scarcely a jolt. He wasn't going to
risk capsizing his boat.

Once in the water, he swam hard to keep up with the
Eline, watching his cousin all the time, and groping under-
water with one hand for the end of the rope. He didn't relax
until the rope was secured around his wrist, and then, realizing that he could come in closer without fouling the rudder,
he shouted to Nicky to slow down while he shortened the
rope a bit. But the *Eline* went faster and faster. Either Nicky
could not hear him, or she could not slacken speed. They
were going so fast now that the rope was cutting into

Matthew's wrist, and he was being dragged along under the water.

When at last he managed to lift his head, he saw that they were heading straight for the rocks of Hollow Tongue. "Nicky, keep to the right!" he yelled. The rudder was jerking from side to side in the water, and she had completely lost control of the boat. "To the right, to the right, I tell you. . . ." The rest of the words were drowned out as another wave washed over his head.

The *Eline* continued on her headlong course, and Matthew realized that their only hope was for him to pull himself alongside and use his weight to bring the boat around.

But he was already exhausted by his efforts to keep up, and by his unavailing shouts to Nicky. His terror that the boat would be smashed on the rocks seemed to be numbing his brain. And suppose Nicky caught sight of the stranger!

"Watch the wind and your helm," Matthew called, so that she would be too busy to look at Hollow Tongue.

If only the stranger would stay hidden.

"Let's moor the boat, so you can come aboard," Nicky shouted to him.

"And be torn to pieces against the rocks?" Matthew shouted back.

Summoning all his strength, he plunged forward, caught hold of the side of the boat, and hung there, hoping desperately that his weight would do the trick, for he was incapable of saying or doing anything more.

Nicky seemed at last to realize what was needed, and

swung the tiller over—in the nick of time. The *Eline* veered
to the right, and came around in a wide curve, just clear of
the rocks. Hollow Tongue was behind them. Matthew
looked around. He did not see anything. The stranger was
still safe.

Now he had to get on board before something else went
wrong. "Hey, Nicky, would you mind giving me a hand?"
he called. She was trembling too much to help him, and he
had to haul himself up. It wasn't easy, but at last he was
back on board. Nicky made room for him, trying not to let
him see the tears of fright in her eyes. Matthew looked
away. He knew she hated anyone to see her crying.

When she had recovered, and he had got his breath back,
he said, "Well, that's learning the hard way."

Nicky replied shakily, "I thought we could land on Hollow Tongue, and you could take over from there."

"Funny way to go about it," said Matthew, adding
hastily as her eyes filled again, "but you did the right thing
in the end. And anyhow, I should have warned you about
those rocks."

"This stupid old boat ought to have had more sense,"
Nicky burst out. They both laughed, and said no more
until the *Eline* was beached on her own side of the bay.

"Well, now I've nearly been on Hollow Tongue myself,"
Nicky said as they hauled the boat on to the blocks. "And
I never realized you were so mad keen on bananas."

"Me? Mad on bananas?" Matthew said in astonishment.
"What on earth are you talking about?"

"Well, how else did all that banana peel get into the water around your island?"

"Oh, I see." Matthew hid his face by ducking behind the boat, pretending to inspect her hull.

"Well, there's no damage," he said when he came up again.

"I only hope no one was watching from the house," Nicky said. "Shall we go and see if tea's ready?" She took a running jump and disappeared behind the mangrove bushes.

Matthew followed her slowly. It had never occurred to him to wonder how the stranger would dispose of the banana peel. If Nicky had noticed it in all the excitement of their near shipwreck, there was no hope that anyone else going near the island would miss it. Not that anyone's likely to go there, Matthew thought. But his thought didn't reassure him.

The rubbish must be got rid of somehow. Obviously, if it were left on the island, the place would be swarming with flies in a day or two. He must tell the stranger to tie it into a bundle with a stone, so that it would sink when he threw it into the sea.

That means I must take him some string tomorrow. His hand was already halfway to his pocket where he usually kept pencil and paper, when he remembered that he was wearing his swimming trunks. No pockets. He started to smile at his own absent-mindedness, but suddenly frowned instead.

Things couldn't go on like this. Someone would notice

soon how oddly he was behaving. The strain of keeping his secret was beginning to get on top of him. If it went on much longer, he'd have to tell somebody, *have* to. He'd shout it for the whole plantation to hear. "The black bird *was* a warning! It's true! There *is* something happening on Hollow Tongue! There's a man there. . . !"

He looked around anxiously, not certain whether he had spoken aloud or not, and caught sight of the island. There was nothing to be seen, no black bird, no stranger. . . . But the man was there all right. Not an ordinary man either, but a fugitive. A jailbird. How could Matthew be sure that he was really a political prisoner, and not just a common criminal? How could he tell, for sure, when he couldn't talk to him? Matthew stamped his foot suddenly, trying to rid himself of the unwelcome thought. He was his friend. He didn't want to think badly of him.

"Hey, Matthew! Where have you been?" Nicky was waving to him from the veranda which ran around the patio.

Matthew was startled by her voice. She sounded so close, and he hadn't even noticed that he was home. What had he been thinking about all this time? The stranger, of course, but before that?

He shut his eyes, trying to remember. Ah yes, string to tie up the banana skins. "String, string, string. . . ." he repeated to himself. "Remember string. . . ."

"Hey, stop talking to yourself! It's the first sign of madness." Standing above him on the veranda, Nicky stretched out her foot to give him a playful kick. Matthew caught hold of her leg. Nicky lost her balance and rolled into the patio. She was up again in a moment and began chasing Matthew. They made so much noise that Paulina rushed out of the kitchen to see what was going on. "Will you behave yourselves. . . !" she shouted, and she grabbed Matthew, who was nearer, and started to shake him furiously. As she shook, her face seemed to get broader and broader and bigger and bigger, until it became the nightmare face of the stranger in his dream last night. Suddenly terrified, Matthew wrenched himself free, shouting in a panic, "Let me go! Let me go!"

Paulina looked at him in astonishment.

Matthew took a deep breath, then turned on his heel and ran into the house. Once in his room, he pushed back the mosquito net and threw himself on his bed.

He touched his forehead and found it was wet. It was hot . . . unbearably hot . . . it would be so much cooler in the bay . . . out in a boat there was always a breeze . . . then he remembered. "No!" he said aloud. He didn't want to go back to the bay. He didn't want to go back to Hollow Tongue, not ever, ever again!

CHAPTER NINE

Footprints in the Sand

"Matthew van Rooy."

Matthew looked up nervously, putting his hand over his exercise book to hide the bird he was drawing.

"Y-yes, sir?"

"Are you feeling all right?" The history master was usually so aloof. Why was he taking so much notice of him this morning?

Matthew found that he could not meet the teacher's eyes.

"Last week I thought you were tired, but perhaps you're feeling the heat. Do you find it oppressive in here?"

Looking straight ahead, Matthew nodded. Mr. Amberg must have noticed something odd about him.

"Go outside for a bit. Put your head under the cold tap and have a drink, and come back when you feel better."

Feeling dazed, Matthew got up from his desk and walked slowly out of the classroom.

Water, he thought longingly, when he was in the corridor. Cool water. But when he thought of water, he couldn't help thinking of the bay. And then of Hollow Tongue.

Even so, he had a drink, then wet his head, and let the water run over his wrists until he felt a little cooler. Then he sat down on a step. The headmaster might come along at any moment, but what did it matter? He'd simply say he was dizzy. And it would be quite true!

Had Mr. Amberg really noticed anything? Grownups always knew when something was wrong. Matthew bent his head and stared at the flagstones at his feet. If you stared long enough, the cracks began to move . . . first slowly . . . then faster . . . right across the slabs . . . just like water. He swayed back and forth, muttering, "Water, water." Then realizing what he was doing, he looked up nervously, afraid that someone might have heard him. But the corridor was empty, threateningly empty, as though it was waiting for someone or something to come.

Someone. But who?

The first form were having a singing lesson. They were singing a French sea chantey about a sailor and his boat. A sailor . . . a seaman . . . the stranger, Matthew thought. He swayed gently in time to the music. It had the same rhythm as the *Eline* when she was sailing calmly across the bay.

"*Il était un petit navire. . . .*" He had always thought it a lovely song, but today it sounded sad. Perhaps because he was feeling sad himself.

It had started when he got into the playground. He was looking for Piet, because he needed to borrow some money. He had long ago spent all his pocket money on things for the stranger, and now he didn't have enough to buy the string. He couldn't open his money box, because someone might notice at home. Piet would lend him the money, but Matthew wanted to get him alone to ask him.

But Piet was in the middle of a noisy group, all talking

at once about the annual school outing, that would be taking place in a few weeks. They usually had a picnic on one of the beaches, and spent the day swimming and sailing. Then in the evening they lit a campfire and sang songs around it.

Piet called to him as soon as he appeared at the gate. "Hallo, Matthew! Have you heard the news? This year's outing is to be at your place. Won't that be marvelous? We'll all be able to sail in your boat!"

"And go to Hollow Tongue!" Tim shouted enthusiastically.

"Showoff! You'd never dare!" Nicky stuck her tongue out at him.

"I would, as long as I wasn't alone! And Matthew's father is arranging to borrow the fishing boats for the day as well." Piet danced with excitement, and slapped Matthew on the back.

"What's the matter with you, Matthew? You don't look very pleased about it," Victor said.

"No . . . I'm just surprised. This is the first I've heard of it." Matthew tried to look unconcerned and to pretend that he was as delighted as the others. But all he could think was, It's all up now.

Suddenly he began to shout. "If my father asks the school to Brakkeput that's one thing, but nobody's going to land on Hollow Tongue!"

There was a shocked silence.

"Anyone would think the island belonged to you," Gerard de Wit said spitefully, and this time, the whole class agreed with him.

"You can say what you like, you're not going there." But as he glared around at their hostile faces, Matthew felt sick at his own helplessness. It was all very well to talk, but what could he do to stop them?

The argument started all over again at break, with Gerard de Wit making the most of his opportunity.

"He just isn't one of us any more," Gerard said at the end. Gerard de Wit, of all people, whom nobody liked, to say things like that about Matthew, and be backed by all the others!

The others flicked notes to each other, and if they caught him looking they shrugged their shoulders and turned away, as if he didn't exist. He knew what being sent to Coventry meant: he had done it to other people, but somehow he had never thought that it might happen to him. If only Father hadn't made that suggestion about the school outing! Brooding on the step, Matthew remembered that the whole idea of inviting his class to Brakkeput had been his own—a long time ago though. Now he groaned at the thought. It was too late to do anything about it, and the picnic was less than three weeks off.

Sixteen days to go, Matthew thought. A lot can happen in that time. And one thing in particular simply had to happen. The stranger must leave Hollow Tongue. But he couldn't get away, not without a boat anyway, and where was he to get a boat?

There were only three boats in Brakkeput: the two fishing boats belonging to Enriqui, Alfredo and Joseph—and his own *Eline*.

"Well, Matthew, are you feeling better now?"

He looked up. The history master was standing at the top of the stairs. Matthew got slowly to his feet.

"I think perhaps I should send you home. You look as if you might be running a fever."

Matthew shook his head. If he didn't go back into class, the others would think he was running away. When he got to his desk, he found that a note had been pushed under his book. At first he pretended not to notice. Then, when he thought no one was watching, he quickly unfolded it and read: "*Who cares about them, anyway. Nicky.*"

He put his hand over the piece of paper so that no one else could see it, and looked around at his cousin. But she was whispering to her neighbor, and pretended not to see him. Matthew felt dejected again. He had thought Nicky was on his side, and now she wouldn't even look at him.

When the bell rang for the end of lessons, Matthew rushed out of the classroom, and was the first to reach the school gates. He was disappointed when he saw that it was Alfredo who had come to fetch him, for, although he wasn't expecting his mother, everything would have been so much easier if she had come. For one thing he would have been able to speak to her about the outing right away.

Alfredo whistled shrilly to hurry him up, but Matthew was not going to be rushed this afternoon. He could hear the others coming up behind him. He didn't have to look around to know they were making faces behind his back. If he went too fast they would think he was running away, and jeer at him.

He was only a few yards from the car now, and he tried to produce a nonchalant whistle, but his mouth was too dry. Well, perhaps he did have a fever, after all.

Alfredo was beckoning impatiently. "I thought you could move faster than that," he said, when Matthew got into the car at last.

"I'm terribly hot, much too hot to run," Matthew said, wiping his wet forehead with the back of his hand.

All the way home Alfredo kept giving him sidelong glances. It made Matthew very uneasy, but there was nothing he could do about it. Alfredo seemed to be in a strange mood altogether.

"They have found the stranger." Matthew sat bolt upright. Had Alfredo said that, or had he himself merely thought it? He didn't know, he just didn't know. In his heart, he hoped it was true. Then it would all be over. There would be nothing more to worry about, and the outing could take place after all. As long as the man didn't give him away, Matthew could pretend he had known nothing about it. But even as he thought what a relief it would be, he reproached himself for being a coward.

"It's going to rain," Alfredo said.

"Good. It's been stifling the last few days," Matthew replied. He could feel the sweat from the back of his neck running down inside his shirt, and more sweat pouring down his forehead. He mopped his brow with a handkerchief.

"This time of year, rain no good," Alfredo mumbled.

They were now driving on a sandy track through a dry

plain. A cloud of dust hovered behind the car and the cacti seemed to be pointing threatening fingers at them.

"Must you drive so fast?" Matthew said to Alfredo, feeling suddenly very unwell.

But Alfredo took no notice. Instead, he kept muttering to himself.

"What are you talking about?" Matthew asked curiously.

"Who, me?" Now it was Alfredo's turn to be startled.

"Yes, you were talking to yourself. What's up?"

"Oh, it's only Enriqui, again." They had come to a bend, and Alfredo took it so sharply that Matthew fell against him. When he had righted himself, Alfredo went on, "Enriqui said this morning a man's been near the boats."

"Someone near the boats?" In a flash Matthew realized what must have happened. The stranger had swum across

Big Mouth during the night, walked along the beach to the creek, and had taken a good look at the Brakkeput fishing boats, to see if he could use one of them to escape.

Thank goodness it's not my boat he's after, Matthew thought. After all, he wouldn't need to swim all that way to look at the *Eline*. He sees her every day, and he must know she's of far less use to him than the larger boats.

Then, aloud, he said, "How did Enriqui find out?"

"Strange footprints in the sand."

"Did he find them around the *Eline* too?" Matthew hoped Alfredo wouldn't realize he was just making conversation; he knew the answer.

"No, not around the *Eline*."

"Perhaps Enriqui imagined the whole thing," Matthew suggested. The men were taking this nocturnal visit much too seriously for his peace of mind. They might even take it into their heads to search the whole bay. Including, perhaps, Hollow Tongue. . . . No, they'd never dare land on the island, Matthew reassured himself. Unless of course they ask Father to help them. If he thought someone was after the fishing boats he'd stop at nothing to catch him, and he's not scared of being swallowed up by ghosts or by black birds. . . .

Alfredo shook his head. "No, Enriqui may be old man, but he no fool. All of us see the footprints. And the black bird."

"The black bird again?" This time Matthew was really frightened.

"Well, not just now, but a few days back." Alfredo must

have seen Matthew's expression, for he smiled slyly. But he soon sobered up again. It was no laughing matter. Strange things were happening, things no one could explain.

Matthew thought of asking whether Enriqui had told Father about the footprints. But there was no sense in putting ideas into Alfredo's head. They rode in silence for a few minutes. Matthew wondered why Alfredo was taking such a long way around, and why he was driving much faster than usual. Father always said that Alfredo was a car fiend, who was only really happy when he was driving like a madman.

"Enriqui says he's going to sleep by boats until it's all over," Alfredo said after a while.

Matthew felt the blood drain from his face, and he shivered in spite of the heat. "Until what is over?" he managed to stammer out. "What does Enriqui think will happen?"

"He thinks somebody going to try and steal the boats," Alfredo said somberly.

"But suppose he's wrong. Is he going to sleep by the boats forever?"

"Don't know," Alfredo shrugged his shoulders.

And as they drove into Brakkeput, he added gravely, "You better watch your *Eline*, I tell you."

At tea, Matthew was so quiet and ate so little that his mother wanted to send him straight up to bed.

"I'm sure you've caught a chill," she said anxiously. Catching cold in the tropics was a serious matter. You were liable to get pneumonia, and in this heat pneumonia was often fatal.

"No," he said. "I'm perfectly all right. I think I'll go for a sail and get some air, though. It's absolutely stifling."

But he wasn't allowed to go out until his mother had taken his temperature. "And you are to come straight back if you don't feel well," she called as he disappeared across the patio. Luckily he had taken extra provisions for the stranger the day before, so he just had to carry his satchel, some bananas, and a bottle of water—nothing unusual or suspicious.

But he knew his mother was anxious. And it wasn't just because she thought he had caught a cold. He realized she had heard about the mysterious footprints, and didn't want to mention it in case he got scared.

CHAPTER TEN

Matthew Decides

Hollow Tongue looked quite deserted. For a moment Matthew thought that the stranger must have made off in the night. He gave a shrill whistle, hoping there would be no answer. If only it were true and the stranger had been to the creek, and had gone around the coast to the next bay to take a boat from there! His arms full, Matthew clambered quickly up the rocks and burst into the tent. It was empty.

But he had hardly had time to put his satchel down when he heard a voice saying, "Hallo." So he had been wrong after all! He had hoped so hard that his troubles were over that for a moment he couldn't answer.

When he finally looked at the stranger, he noticed that the man was looking very cheerful. He knows that there's a chance of getting away in one of the boats from Brakke-put, Matthew thought. But it couldn't be the *Eline*. The man wouldn't have the heart, after all Matthew had done for him. He just couldn't do a thing like that. But the more he told himself it was impossible, the less certain he became.

Had the man noticed something was up? Suddenly he began to speak as he had never spoken before. To Matthew, it was all a confused babble, for the man was chattering in a mixture of Spanish and English with a few Dutch words thrown in. But he managed to make out that the man had seen the boats in the creek; that his wife and two sons were

114

waiting for him at home . . . they hadn't seen him for so long, they must think he was dead . . . he simply must get back to them.

Matthew just nodded, without saying a word. There was no need to say anything. He knew what the man wanted. And what could Matthew do about it anyway?

He should warn him that Enriqui intended to spend the next few nights watching by the boats. But if he said that, the man would take the *Eline*. He must beach the *Eline* in the creek, so that the man couldn't get at her. But then, how would the stranger get away? And what about his wife and children? They were waiting. . . . Matthew tried to imagine his own father, stranded on a lonely island, far from home, just like the stranger. . . .

"When are you going?" Matthew asked very slowly.

The man shrugged his shoulders.

Hasn't he made up his mind yet? Or doesn't he trust me? Matthew thought. He felt a dull pain, a pain that seemed to come from nowhere in particular, but that was there all the same. He rested his head on his knees—he didn't want the man to see his face.

Suddenly, he felt the stranger's hand on his head. He stayed quite still, and the hand stroked his hair, then his face, and finally lifted his chin. Now he couldn't help looking up.

"Not your boat," the man said in English, and smiled.

He's not taking the *Eline*, he's not taking the *Eline*! Matthew could have shouted for joy.

But his happiness didn't last long. For, if the stranger didn't take the *Eline*, he would take one of the natives' boats.

Through the open tent flap, Matthew looked across the bay. He couldn't see the boats in the creek, but he could imagine them lying there peacefully, not suspecting that anything was amiss. Or could a boat sense that something was going to happen to it? Just as you yourself sensed when something was in the air. Suppose the man really did manage to steal one?

"You know," he stammered out, "Enriqui's and Alfredo's and Joseph's boats aren't just ordinary boats. The three of them had to work terribly hard to save up enough money for them. And Joseph's and Alfredo's boat is the only thing they've got. They have absolutely nothing else, and their whole family, even the ones in Santa Cruz, have to live on what they earn by fishing. There's no money except what Enriqui, Alfredo and Joseph get for their fish, and if anything happened to the boats . . ."

It didn't matter now whether the man had understood or not. At last, Matthew himself had realized what it would mean if the stranger took one of the natives' boats. The man went to the back of the tent, and lit a cigarette. Matthew felt the spent match fly past his head. There was not a sound in the tent. And it was hot, stifling hot.

It's going to rain, Matthew thought. He looked at the roof of the tent. On Curaçao it didn't rain often. But when it did rain, it was usually a cloudburst. The tent wouldn't stand up to it. Perhaps it would be swept away, and then everyone would be able to see the stranger. Then all his trouble would have been for nothing. The man would be recognized at once, for the "Wanted" notices with the names of the fugitives from Uquique were still stuck up all over the island. Everybody pretended not to have heard of Dr. Van Boom's rescue party.

It's all very well for them, but I am right in the middle of it, Matthew thought miserably. The tent would be blown away in a storm, and the man would be sent back to prison in spite of everything. There he sat with not the slightest idea that it was going to rain. How lucky he was! *He* didn't have to think about the rain, or about the school outing, or about how terrible it would be if one of the natives' boats were stolen!

But when he turned around, Matthew realized that the stranger was staring hard at him. And he went on staring. He was holding the cigarette in one hand and smoothing the mattress with the other.

I wonder what he's thinking about, Matthew asked himself. The air mattress, could that mean anything?

Then, suddenly, he realized what hardships the stranger was facing. A long, long journey with little food and little water. And then the scorching sun for days on end! And no one to help him with the sailing. And always the chance of being picked up by a police patrol if he came too close to the coast.

And when he finally reached his own country, would he be really safe even then? Wouldn't they just be waiting for him, to lock him up? He couldn't even be sure that his family were still there.

Matthew crept out of the tent, dropped down from the rock, untied the *Eline* and sailed straight for the beach. As if in a dream, he pulled his boat up on to dry land, and sat down on the sand stroking her smooth hull.

Only when it began to get dark, and Enriqui suddenly appeared at his side, did he realize where he was, and how late it must be.

How could the time have gone so fast?

"Your mother is worried," Enriqui said.

Matthew got up. His legs were stiff from sitting still for so long. He began to speak, then shut his mouth tight. He had made his decision. And it was nobody else's business.

"You don't mind, do you, if we go out to see Aunt Else?"

It was the third time his mother had asked him, and for the third time Matthew said, "Yes, yes, do go. I'm quite all right, really."

"If you don't feel well, give us a ring at once, won't you?" Mother said before she got into the car.

"Don't worry too much, Paulina is here after all," Father told her.

Matthew waved to them from the veranda. Now there was only Paulina left, but she would keep indoors all the time. He'd just have to sneak off, and hope she wouldn't notice that he'd gone. It was a risk, because it was so late, and she might easily come and look for him, but there was nothing else he could do.

For the last time, he crept into the larder to see what food he could take for the stranger. Bananas in any case, they were better than nothing, even though the man had almost been living on them. What else?

"Hey, what do you think you're doing?" Paulina had heard him.

"Just seeing if there's anything nice to eat," Matthew called back. Mother had told him he could help himself whenever he felt like it, so Paulina couldn't really say anything. As long as she didn't come and investigate.

He listened for her shuffling in the passage, but luckily

she did not appear. Quickly he lifted the covers of all the boxes and barrels. When he left the larder, he was carrying three bags of provisions. Now for the water.

But that wasn't going to be so easy. If he took all the bottles from the refrigerator, Paulina was bound to hear him, and then he'd have to explain what he was going to do with all that water. He shot back into the larder, took a new shopping bag, and packed it with Coca-Cola bottles. There was a can opener on Hollow Tongue.

He looked around the shelves to see if he had forgotten anything. But he could think of nothing more. Then he slipped out of the larder, through the back of the house, and across the patio toward the plantation. The four bags were as heavy as lead, and he wondered whether the handles would last until he got to the beach.

Matthew kept looking around to see if anyone was about. Brakkeput seemed full of mysterious noises and unexpected shadows. When a ripe medlar shot past his head as it fell from the tree, he got such a fright that he began to run. Only when he reached the mangrove bushes did he slacken his pace.

Watch out for the hornets! And for Enriqui! If Enriqui was down at the creek, he was sure to see him. But the beach was empty and no one spotted him pushing the *Eline* into the water and sailing across the bay.

As he brought the dinghy about on the far side of Hollow Tongue, Matthew remembered his first visit to the island. How he wished that he had never landed!

To his surprise, the stranger was waiting for him. Silently the man helped him to make fast.

Matthew stepped ashore, looking hard at the man, and
hoping he would be able to make him understand why he
had come. He went into the tent while the man followed
him slowly.

"You simply mustn't take any of the natives' boats. You
just can't. You must take my boat. You must escape in my
boat." Then he waited for the man's reply.

"No," said the man dully, "no."

"Yes, yes, you must go, do you hear me, you must go.

You can't stay here any longer. They'll find you. If the rains start, and the school outing . . ." Matthew suddenly stopped talking, realizing that the man couldn't possibly understand what he was saying.

"Not your boat," the man said fiercely, in English.

Perhaps he thinks she's too small, Matthew thought suddenly. He looked at the stranger with dismay. Could it be that?

"My boat is just as good as the others," he said persuasively. "I've brought you food and drink, and you must take the tent and the air mattress and the eiderdown. Everything!" He didn't wait for the man to reply. He had made his decision and the sooner it was carried out the better.

With an air of finality he picked up the mattress and dragged it out of the tent.

"Hey!" the man called out.

"Sshhh," Matthew whispered back.

The man followed him out and together they put the mattress into the dinghy and then went back for the food. The box Matthew had brought to sit on just fitted in nicely.

They had to grope in the dark to find all the things, but the hardest part was taking down the tent.

"Don't let them see us, please don't let them see us!" Matthew prayed. The sun had gone down, and the trade wind was blowing across the bay, but he felt just as hot as he had in the afternoon. Until everything was safely stowed away, he hardly dared to breathe. Then, together, they stood by the *Eline*, the stranger and he. They did not dare look at each other, for neither knew what to say.

"I'll take her clear of Hollow Tongue. Then I'll jump overboard and swim to the beach," Matthew said at last. But as he turned to get in the boat, the man put his arm around his shoulders, and hugged him tight. Matthew felt the quick thudding of the man's heart and noticed that his arm was shaking.

"I'm sure you'll get home safely," he said shyly. "I'm sure of it. The *Eline* is a terrific boat."

The man took his arm away. Quickly Matthew jumped in, and waited for the stranger to come aboard. He loosened the painter, and pulled the fenders in. The stranger cast off, and in a few seconds they were clear of Hollow Tongue.

Matthew was holding the tiller and the sheet. He steered the boat in the direction of Brakkeput. "Now," he said, and beckoned to the man. Then he shifted from his place and let the stranger take over. Though it was dark, he could see the man's hands grasp the tiller and pick up the sheet.

"You must go in that direction," Matthew pointed. The stranger nodded.

"Well . . . well, I'm off."

And before the man had a chance to reply, Matthew had jumped overboard.

"Good luck," he said as he came up, and then he raced toward the beach like one possessed. He had at least four hundred yards to go. Not very far, but if there were sharks at night! There was no one to come to his rescue, either.

He would have liked to look around to see how the *Eline* was doing, but it was more than he dared do. Faster, faster! "More to the left," he whispered to himself. If he didn't

watch out, he'd come up by the creek, and Enriqui might
be there!

Just a few strokes more. There was the block where the
Eline used to rest. How far would she have gone by now?
Would she be out of Enriqui's sight if he was watching
from the creek?

The beach! At last! Exhausted, Matthew let himself be
carried ashore by the waves. He was quite spent. All he
wanted was to drop on the sand. But Enriqui might come
along at any moment, and whatever happened, he mustn't
be seen here tonight. No one must have the slightest inkling
that he knew anything about the disappearance of the *Eline*.

He put on his gym shoes, which he'd tucked under his
belt. The water was dripping from his clothes. He must
take care not to leave a telltale trail.

As the first light broke through the shutters, and the birds
began to sing, Matthew jumped out of bed. He had not slept
all night, though he'd pretended to be asleep when Mother
had come to look at him on her return.

No one had noticed anything. Paulina had no idea that
he had been out of the house. Nor Enriqui. Otherwise he
would certainly have told Paulina.

Carefully, Matthew took fresh clothes out of his drawer.
The ones he wore last night were lying all crumpled across
the chair. They smelled of sea water. Thank goodness
Mother hadn't spotted them last night! Where could he
hide them quickly? Wait. He opened the shutters, and
spread them out in the sun. Once they were dry, they could

go in with the rest of the laundry, and no one would be any the wiser.

Matthew leaned on the window sill, looking out at the plantation. Wasn't Brakkeput lovely so early in the morning? The air was still cool and fresh, and the bay in the distance looked as calm and peaceful as if nothing at all had happened.

What would the islanders say when they found out that the *Eline* had disappeared? Simply that Big Mouth had swallowed up one more boat!

And what would they say when they saw that the tent on Hollow Tongue had vanished? Just what they always said, "Everything drops right through Hollow Tongue and sinks to the bottom of the sea."

Well, let them chatter. He would even agree with them. It was far less dangerous than the truth.

I wonder where the stranger has got to by this time? Matthew thought. "The stranger." How silly...! He didn't even know his name.

If only the stranger was careful to keep clear of the rocks just past the creek. That was a dangerous spot. He should have warned him about it. What if the *Eline* was stranded just off the shore?

But when he walked along the beach a little later, the *Eline* was nowhere to be seen. Only the empty block on which she had always lain.

Matthew looked across at Hollow Tongue as he lay on the sand. The rock looked quite bare now that the tent was gone. From a distance, his tent had always looked like a little hat.

Once upon a time Hollow Tongue had been an unexplored island. Once upon a time—but it wasn't long ago. Only just before his birthday.

When his parents gave him the *Eline*, they had really given him Hollow Tongue as well. An island all to himself. All that was over now. And the *Eline* . . ?

He didn't want to look at the empty block, but he could not help doing it. If you closed your eyes tight, you could imagine that the dinghy was still lying on the beach, glistening golden brown in the sun. He could still see the tiller as it had been on his birthday, garlanded with medlar leaves.

Matthew opened his eyes again. He was horrified to see that he had absent-mindedly written "Eline" in the sand. He stared at the letters as if in a dream.

Then he heard the voices of the men, coming up behind him, and smoothed the sand with his hand.

Well, here they were!

It was all over now. He straightened up, and stood defiantly, almost proudly, as they saw the *Eline* was gone.

ABOUT THE AUTHOR

Miep Diekmann was born in Assen, Holland. Her father was a military officer and so she moved about a great deal during her childhood, and for a time lived on the island of Curaçao in the West Indies. Before World War II, Miss Diekmann returned to Holland and continued her studies there. After graduating from the gymnasium (secondary school), she began working in journalism, and published her first novel at the age of twenty-two. She then became interested in writing for young people and published THE HAUNTED ISLAND, which was cited as the best children's book in 1957 in Holland.

Miss Diekmann draws much upon her childhood experience in the West Indies for the characters and setting of her books. Most of the events in THE HAUNTED ISLAND are historical and took place before World War II. In 1958 Miss Diekmann was chosen by the Dutch Merchant Navy to write a book about life at sea, and she returned to the West Indies, renewing old contacts and lecturing at the West Indies schools, where she found that her books were the only ones that the children had about their own islands and lives. In 1961 Miss Diekmann was commissioned by the Antillian Government to write a series of schoolbooks about life on the Leeward Islands. Miss Diekmann and her two children live at The Hague, in Holland.